A PERMANENT MARK

H.K. CHRISTIE

This is a work of fiction. Names, characters, businesses, places, events and incidents are either the products of the author's imagination or used in a fictitious manner. Any resemblance to actual persons, living or dead, or actual events is purely coincidental.

Cover design by Suzana Stankovic

First edition: February 2020

ISBN-13: 978-0-9982856-6-5

ALSO BY H.K. CHRISTIE

The Selena Bailey Series is a suspenseful series featuring a young Selena Bailey and her turbulent path to becoming a top notch kickass private investigator.

Not Like Her, Book 1

One In Five, Book 2

On The Rise, Book 3

The Unbreakable Series is a heart-warming women's fiction series, inspired by true events. If you like journeys of self-discovery, wounded heroines, and laugh-or-cry moments, you'll love the Unbreakable series.

We Can't Be Broken, Book 0

Where I'm Supposed To Be, Book 1

Change of Plans, Book 2

CHAPTER ONE

IRWIN

Irwin sucked the last drag of his Marlboro before flicking it out the car window. He muttered, "Jesus Christ, it's cold," before rolling the window back up. He leaned back in the seat and tilted his head. If this guy didn't show up soon, he'd freeze his balls off. He was getting way too old for this shit. He caught a flicker in the corner of his eye. Adrenaline soaring, he sat up and stared ahead. *Bingo.*

He cranked the engine, and the motor roared. *Damn this old heap,* he thought. It was loud as all get out. *Fingers crossed that none of these nice folks awaken from their safe little beds. Safe. Ha.*

He released the parking brake and headed down the winding road toward the lone runner. Why the hell anybody would wake up before the sun to go for a run was beyond him. Irwin himself had to be in tip-top shape in his line of work, but you'd never catch him running on a pitch-black road in the middle of winter. That was nuts. Didn't this guy realize how unsafe it was to be running along a winding road, in the dark? *Exercise'll kill ya.* He chuckled at his own joke.

Not that Irwin enjoyed taking a life; it was simply a means

to an end. Irwin didn't know anything about this guy. Maybe he was a saint? A sinner? All Irwin knew was that he ran every day, lived in a fancy neighborhood, and had a hot wife who left the house at five in the morning like clockwork. That, and someone wanted him dead.

He gripped the steering wheel and eased along the curve in the road. The jogger in dark clothing, with reflective bands at the ankle and wrists, inched closer to the shoulder. Irwin shook his head and accelerated. "Sorry, man. There isn't a shoulder big enough to help you today." Irwin swerved to the right and gunned the engine.

Upon impact, Irwin instinctively slammed on the brakes and his head flung forward, hitting the windshield. Stunned, Irwin lifted his thick fingers to his head and glanced up in the rearview mirror. *Fuck.* He hadn't expected such an impact. He'd never done a hit-and-run job. He preferred a neat, quiet shot to the skull as they slept, but his employer insisted it had to look like an accident, and for what he was being paid, he was willing to get a little messy. But god damn, no fucking shoulder belts. He was really starting to hate this fucking car. He gave himself a moment before looking up ahead. There was no sign of the jogger or anyone else in or near the road. *Shit.* He had to make sure it was done. Where did he go? Irwin slid over to the passenger side and studied the scene below. The target had been knocked down the side of the hill, completely out of sight from the road. He shook his head. *Damn. It's my lucky day. It'll be hours if not days before they find the sucker down there. Time to get the fuck out of here.*

Back behind the wheel, he drove steadily down the winding, tree-lined road until he hit the intersection at the bottom of the hill. He eased onto the feeder and entered the freeway. He then reached for his pack of smokes and balanced the wheel on his thigh as he lit one up. He took a drag and exhaled a series of smoke rings and then went for the radio knob and stopped. *Piece of shit.* He'd forgotten it didn't even have a working radio.

He drove in silence for thirty minutes before pulling off the highway. He was nearly free and clear. As long as some asshole hadn't been awakened by the crash, he was out of the danger zone. That's all he needed, was to spend the rest of his life in prison on what was to be his last job. He'd been in the game too long, he knew that. He was ready for retirement. Once he got paid, it was adios America and hola Mexico. He could practically taste the salt rim on the margarita.

Now on city streets, he veered his car to the right and entered a residential neighborhood loaded with dilapidated houses and more than a few driveways littered with cars on cinderblocks. *Yep, this piece of crap fits right in.* He eased off the gas and parked at the end of the street. He exited the vehicle, tossed his cigarette on the pavement, and stomped on it with the heel of his shoe.

He hurried to the corner until he reached his shiny, black sedan. Glad to be rid of the old heap of junk, he climbed into the driver's seat, pulled off his gloves, and retrieved the burner from his glovebox. He flipped it open and tapped out a message. *It's done.*

CHAPTER TWO

KENDALL

Kendall grinned as she exited her boss's office at Bay Star Investments. She'd just landed a twenty-million-dollar investment account to manage. It was the largest account she'd been tasked with managing in her twelve-year career in finance, and she knew just the fund to put it in. Maybe one day she'd have a corner office with views of the San Francisco Bay. She continued past the cluster of gray cubicles and lower-level employees, catching a whiff of freshly brewed espresso and determination as she headed toward her tiny office. At least it was an office, one she'd worked her butt off to get.

Two steps from the entrance to her office, she felt the buzz of her cell phone. She pulled it from inside her blazer pocket and glanced at the screen. Her grin widened. "This is a nice surprise." Instead of George's voice, there was static and what sounded like commotion in the background. Commotion that she wasn't familiar with. "George?"

An unfamiliar man's voice asked, "Is this Kendall Davis?"

Her heart raced. "This is Kendall Murphy. Davis is my husband's last name. Who is this? Why do you have George's phone? Where's George?"

What was going on? Kendall stared into her office as if she had entered an alternate universe.

"Ms. Murphy, my name is Detective Rogers with the Ridgemont Police Department. Is your husband George Crawford Davis?"

Kendall put her arm on the metal doorframe of her office, steadying herself. Why did the police have George's phone, asking if George was her husband?

She swallowed. "Yes, George is my husband. What's going on? Why do you have his phone? What's happening?"

"Your husband was in an accident, he—"

"What do you mean? What kind of accident?" She cut off the detective as panic flooded her.

"Your husband was found this morning, unconscious and down an embankment off of Woodmill Drive. One of your neighbors was walking his dog and found him; he recognized George and called 9-1-1. It looks like he may have been the victim of a hit-and-run accident. He was transported to County General Hospital."

Panic shot through her veins. "Is he okay?"

"They're not quite sure of the full extent of your husband's injuries at this time. When they found him, he was unconscious so they rushed him to County General. They suspect some internal injuries but don't know for sure. Do you need the address to the hospital?"

She hurried over to her desk chair, sat down, and with shaking hands, grabbed a yellow sticky note. "No, I know where it is. I'll leave now." She paused. "Shit. I'm in San Francisco, but traffic should be okay at this hour. Is there a phone number I can call to get the updated information on how he's doing?" Her mind was racing, making it difficult to focus.

"I just spoke with the hospital, but I can give you the main line to the hospital as well as my cell number. My partner and I will be at the hospital when you arrive. I think it would be best if you come as soon as possible."

Kendall sunk into her chair. *It's best that I come down to the hospital as soon as possible? He's unconscious. Maybe it's just a concussion. It can't be more than that, right?* Why did he always insist on running when it was dark out? He'd finally placated her and agreed to always carry his cell phone in the event he ran into any trouble. He had to be okay. He had to.

"I'm sorry, what was the number again?"

The detective repeated himself, and she scribbled the digits on the sticky note. "I'll pack up and leave now."

"Drive safe."

Her heart pounded in her ears. "Thanks."

She breathed deeply and counted to ten. At ten, she grabbed her purse and stormed out of her office.

KENDALL RUSHED THROUGH THE AUTOMATIC DOORS INTO the emergency room of County General and was assaulted with the smell of antibacterial soap and bleach. She marched up to the reception and proclaimed, "Hi, my name is Kendall Murphy and I'm here to see my husband, George Davis. Please direct me to his room." She knew she was speaking a mile a minute, but she couldn't help it. She needed to see George. *Now.*

"How do you spell that?"

Kendall wanted to smack the woman. How do you spell that? George fucking Davis. For the love of god, they were only two of the most common names in the universe.

"George G-E-O-R-G-E Davis D-A-V-I-S." God, she hoped this wasn't the person who was in charge of taking care of her husband.

Kendall tapped a middle finger against her thigh, calming

herself with repetitive motion as the woman who seemed to be unable to spell commonly spelled names peered at her computer monitor.

George will be okay. George will be okay. George will be okay. He had to be okay. There was no world of hers in which George wasn't okay. He could recover from a concussion or other common internal injuries, like a busted spleen, right? *Do people even need a spleen?*

The woman with a round face and smudged glasses glanced up from her computer. "Your husband's in surgery right now. Take a seat and wait for the doctor to come out to talk to you."

"Surgery? When did he go into surgery?"

"Ma'am, I don't have all the details. You'll have to wait for the doctor to come out, okay?"

Frustrated, Kendall was about to storm off when she nearly stumbled into a boyish-looking man, wearing a crumpled navy suit, standing behind her. "Kendall Murphy?"

She recognized the voice from George's phone. Her heart sank. "Yes."

He extended his hand. "My name is Detective Rogers, and this is my partner, Detective Gates."

Detective Gates was at least ten years older than his partner, with kind, hazel eyes. She shook both their hands absent-mindedly. "What's happening with George? They just told me that he was in surgery. Why is he in surgery?"

Detective Rogers spoke in even tones. "Ms. Murphy, they took him into surgery about forty-five minutes ago. We're waiting for the doctor to come out and tell us how he's doing. We don't know how long it'll be. Maybe it's best we take a seat. Is that okay?"

Kendall shrugged as she followed them over to the first row of dingy, brown chairs. She sat and stared off into nowhere. Detective Rogers said, "I know this is a rough time—you're probably worried sick about your husband, understandably—but it could really help us if we could ask you a few questions to find out what happened to George."

Kendall mumbled, "Yeah, sure."

The detective started, "How long . . ." and then stopped.

Kendall looked over her shoulder to understand why he had paused mid-sentence. She froze at the sight of the approaching doctor in green scrubs and a face mask pulled below her chin. Even with a stoic expression, the doctor couldn't hide the look of defeat in her eyes.

Kendall's heart slowed.

No, this wasn't a movie. There wouldn't be a sad shake of the head by the surgeon indicating the worst, followed by 'We did everything we could.' This was real life, scenes like those didn't really happen. Did they?

Kendall and the detectives stood. Detective Rogers nodded his head toward Kendall and said, "Doctor Zemeni, this is Kendall Murphy, George's wife."

The doctor nodded.

Kendall blurted, "How is he? Is he awake? Can I see him now?"

The surgeon's face remained expressionless. "Your husband sustained massive internal injuries. Initially, we were hopeful that we could stop some of the bleeding and repair the damage. He suffered a lot of trauma from the accident. We did everything we could, but I'm afraid it wasn't enough. We couldn't save him. I'm sorry for your loss."

All the air escaped Kendall's lungs, and her knees buckled; detective Rogers caught her before she could fall. Kendall shook her head. "No, no, this can't be right. It's not my George." Her muscles tensed, and her adrenaline flared. "This has to be a mistake! Let me see him. This, this can't be happening." She squeezed the detective's arms, which were still holding her, and pleaded. "No, this is, no, no, he's not gone."

The surgeon spoke in a flat voice. "I'm very sorry for your loss." She eyed the detectives before shuffling back down the corridor.

Tears dripped off Kendall's chin, and the detective released his grip, helping her sit down.

"This can't be. This can't be right. Are you sure it was him? I mean, yes, you had his phone, but maybe he just dropped it and it fell near this other person. There are a lot of runners in our neighborhood. It could have been anyone. Have you tried calling George at work?" Kendall pulled out her phone and fumbled with it as she attempted to call George's office.

Detective Rogers explained, "George's driver's license was tucked inside the case of his cell phone, the ID matches, and your neighbor recognized him. We are confident it is George, although we will need you to officially identify him, also."

The older detective held up a plastic evidence bag containing a wide silver-toned wedding band with a Celtic design. Tears spilled from Kendall's eyes. She placed her hand on her chest and hunched over as she sobbed in front of the now-quiet detectives.

Detective Rogers handed her a white tissue. She stared at it as if it were a foreign object from another planet. A planet where nothing made sense. A planet where George was gone. She didn't want to be on this planet.

She wiped her face and more tissues appeared. When she'd composed herself, Detective Rogers said, "When you're ready we can go see George."

She would never be ready to see her husband's lifeless body.

She quietly counted to ten, and said, "I'm ready."

The men escorted Kendall into the surgery suite, where George lay still. A hospital blanket was pulled all the way up to his chin, covering the majority of him. She reached out her hand and touched his cheek. He was still warm. And beautiful, even with the bruising. She leaned over to embrace him one last time and the sobs returned. At that moment, she felt something inside of her break.

From over her shoulder, she heard, "Is there someone we can call for you?"

She stood up and spoke softly. "My sister, Janine. Janine Murphy." With her eyes fixed on George, she pulled her phone from her back pocket and handed it to the detective without looking.

She didn't know how much time had passed before she heard Janine call out her name. She stood rigidly as her little sister embraced her. She cried, "Janine. He's gone. He's really gone."

More tissues came from somewhere. She was a mess. She told herself to pull it together. She stepped back and wiped her face with the back of her hand. It wasn't fair. She'd lost her parents and now her husband. She darted her eyes over to the detectives. Rage soared through her. "You will find the person who did this, right?"

Detective Rogers nodded. "I will do everything in my power to find who did this to your husband. You have my word."

Kendall accepted his promise and grabbed Janine's hand. She bowed her head as she walked out of what was now the worst place she'd ever visited.

CHAPTER THREE

MARCUS

Marcus Rogers slid into the driver's seat of their police-issued sedan and shut the door. Before Marcus had a chance to start the car, Gates said, "Making promises to the widow is the kind of crap that'll come back to bite you—and hard. What the hell were you thinking?"

Marcus knew better than to make promises, but the devastation in Kendall's bright green eyes made him realize that not only did he want to solve the case, he had to. For her. He hadn't seen that kind of grief in a long time.

He could still vividly recall the look in his own mother's eyes when they'd discovered his youngest brother was missing. Behind his mother's grief and anguish, there lay a spark of hope that Shawn would come home. Kendall's eyes had no spark. No hope. Just sadness, devastation, and anger.

He had to find George Davis's killer. If he didn't find the person or persons responsible, it would haunt him. As it was, he barely slept; ever since Shawn had disappeared more than fifteen years ago, his nights were filled with nothing but bad dreams.

Marcus started the engine. "We'll catch him. In that neighborhood, there are multiple homes with security cameras. We'll review the tapes and find the car. Likely it was an accident by some reckless teens or someone coming off a late shift who didn't get enough sleep."

Gates slipped on his sunglasses. "I hope you're right. Let's start knocking on doors and get the footage."

"I'll begin looking at footage tonight. We'll get this guy and fast—before the perp gets a chance to fix the car."

"Not a bad plan, buddy, but I have to say, you gotta get a life. If you spend all your days and nights on the job, it'll chew you up and spit you out. It'll drive you crazy. I see it happen a lot with rookies."

Marcus's blood pressure spiked. "I'm not a rookie. I've been doing this for six years and—"

"Yeah, you've been on the force for six years, but you've been a detective less than a year. Sorry, buddy, that makes you a rookie. This job is different than being on patrol. This is a whole new world here. That stuff we saw back at the hospital becomes part of your life. You gotta find a way to compartmentalize. Don't let this job break you. Trust me. Go find you a young thing. Have some fun. Chicks love cops, especially detectives. If I were single, I'd be out there getting tail every night. Shoot, you're a good-lookin' guy. What are you waiting for?"

Marcus thought about what his partner said. He knew he needed to get out more. But ever since he made detective, he was determined to rise up in the ranks. He wanted to earn respect and influence so he could run his own investigations and be able to actively work his brother's missing person's case.

They hadn't ever found out what happened to Shawn. They didn't know if he was alive, being held captive, or dead, but Marcus was determined to find out the truth. If he had the clout, he could reopen the case. So, if he had to work day and night to get it, that was exactly what he'd do.

But first he had to find George Davis's killer and bring justice and closure for Kendall. He wondered why Kendall had made such an impression on him. He didn't know if it was because she was young and beautiful, or if it was because there was something about her determination when she demanded that they find George's killer. He didn't know what it was, but there was something about Kendall Murphy that he couldn't shake.

MARCUS WAS HUNCHED OVER HIS LAPTOP COMPUTER WHEN Gates approached with a couple of coffees and a white paper bag displaying the telltale grease stain of donuts. The scent of strong coffee and fresh baked goods made his stomach rumble.

Gates dropped the bag on the desk. "Hey there, buddy. I hope you weren't here all night, but from the looks of you—which, by the way, you look like shit—it seems you were. Please tell me you found something."

Marcus's bloodshot eyes widened, and he pushed off his seat. "Hell yeah. I've got a make and model of the old clunker that passed by at 6:05 a.m. right in front of the scene of the accident. Strange thing is that there's no license plate, but there are only a few 1979 Lincoln Town Cars in light blue registered in the San Francisco Bay Area. I have a list of addresses. You and I are knocking on some doors and catching the asshole *today*."

Gates sunk into his chair. "Buddy, you have too much energy. Can I have my coffee first?"

Marcus waved his hands in the air above his head, making his six-foot frame seem much bigger. "Seriously? You can drink your coffee in the car. I'll drive."

Gates hoisted himself out of the desk chair. "Okay. Okay.

Let's catch the S.O.B, but maybe you lay off the caffeine—and I'll drive."

Marcus popped a glazed old-fashioned in his mouth and nodded. He could feel it in his gut: they were close.

Adrenaline pumping and heart racing, Marcus studied the neighborhood as they approached the first address on the list. It was an older neighborhood with small ranch-style homes and modest cars parked in driveways. Not a luxury vehicle in sight. The house was small, with a one-car garage and white paint peeling off. In the driveway was a light blue 1979 Lincoln Town Car matching the description of the vehicle in question. It was covered in a layer of dirt with cinder blocks behind the rear wheels.

The detectives approached the front door and knocked. Nobody answered. Gates knocked again. Marcus heard shuffling from the other side of the door. When it opened, there stood a woman in her eighties, wearing a housecoat and slippers. She said, "Hello. What can I help you with?"

"Hello, ma'am, my name is Detective Rogers, and this is my partner, Detective Gates. We have a few questions for you about the vehicle in the driveway." He thumbed over his shoulder. "Is that your car?"

The woman edged forward and peered over at the driveway, as if she wasn't sure what car he was referring to. She said, "Oh, that car used to be my husband's. It hasn't seen much action lately. My husband passed a few years back. I never could bring myself to part with the car. My grandson was thinking of maybe fixing it up. He's almost sixteen now. But he hasn't been by much, maybe he doesn't want it after all."

"Do you mind if we take a look at the car?" Marcus asked.

The woman said, "I can't see why not. Go ahead. What are you looking for anyhow?"

Gates interjected. "There was a vehicle matching the description of the one you have in the driveway that was involved in a hit-and-run accident. Chances are it was a completely different car, but we have to make sure. You know, dotting our i's and crossing our t's. It's nothing to worry about, we'll be out of your hair in no time."

She retreated back into the house. "Oh, okay. Let me know if you need anything. I'm gonna put on some tea. Can I get you gentleman any?"

"No, thank you, ma'am."

Gates and Marcus sauntered over to the vehicle in the driveway. They inspected it for any recent damage. With the amount of trauma caused to George's body and remnants at the scene, it was likely there would be damage to the hood, the headlights, and the fender. Maybe even the wheels.

Gates put his fist on his hips and said, "I don't see any damage here, buddy. I think we can cross this one off our list."

Marcus deflated. "I agree. Let's move on to the next one."

They pulled up to the next address on their list, not spotting the car in the driveway, but that didn't mean anything. It could easily be in the garage, which would make more sense; if you'd committed a hit-and-run, you'd want to keep it hidden, not have it sitting out in the open.

They knocked on the door and waited. Gates and Marcus exchanged glances before Marcus knocked on the door once again. They were about to turn around and walk off when the door creaked open. In the doorway stood a man not a day under ninety. He was tall but hunched over with crepe-like skin and bony fingers. He raised his skeleton-like arm. "Hey, there."

Gates approached the man. "Hello, sir, my name is Detective Gates. This is my partner Detective Rogers. We are here because we're investigating an accident with a vehicle, one that matches the description of a car registered to you. Do you have a car?"

"Why yes, I do. It's right there in the driveway. Don't you see it?"

Gates and Marcus exchanged glances.

"No, sir, there's not a car in the driveway. Are you sure that's where you parked it?"

"Sure, I'm sure." The old man crept out of his house at a snail's pace, bending over even further to catch a glimpse of his empty driveway. He turned back toward the detectives. "Well, I'll be. It was right there. I don't know where it went."

"Is there any chance you parked it in the garage and don't remember?" Gates asked.

"Oh no, I don't think so. My garage is full of so much junk, I couldn't get a bicycle in there, let alone a car. Someone must have stolen my car. Can you believe it? I'll tell you what. It runs like a beauty, that car. I've kept it up myself for the last forty years. Original owner. Now some hooligans went off and took it!"

Marcus asked, "Sir, do you want to make a police report for your stolen vehicle?"

He stared into Marcus's eyes. "What did you say, son?"

Marcus leaned forward and raised his voice, repeating himself.

With a nod of the head, the old man smiled. "Of course! I guess I'm lucky you two stopped by—saved me a phone call."

How likely is it that the same make and model for a forty-year-old car was involved in a hit-and-run and is now being reported stolen? Something in his gut told him they were getting close. But the fact that it was a stolen vehicle wouldn't make it any easier to find.

With the details of the stolen vehicle written up, the detectives jumped back in their own car. Gates smirked. "There's thirty minutes of my life I'll never get back. Yikes."

"It was mentally painful, but I'm glad we had a chance to look around. The old guy doesn't hear very well, which means it would've been easy to swipe the car. I've got a feeling his car is the one we're looking for."

"I think you're right. Some punk kids, probably all hopped up on god-knows-what, took it for a joyride and accidentally hit George Davis. You, my friend, may be able to keep the promise you made to the widow, and quickly, but let's cover our asses and get through the rest of that list."

"Agreed. I'll put out a BOLO on the car while we hit the other addresses. And hopefully, the traffic cam footage comes in soon so we can see where it went after the accident."

Marcus could taste how close they were to finding the perp. But he wasn't convinced it was kids out for a joyride; the video showed someone had removed the license plates. Why would kids do that if they were just fooling around? He didn't think it was kids, but he did think someone took that old man's car and used it in the accident that caused George Davis's death—and he was going to prove it.

CHAPTER FOUR

IRWIN

Irwin was lounging in his recliner, smoking a cig and watching a replay of the Raider's game, when his phone rang. He glanced at the screen. *It's about fucking time.* He answered, "Yeah."

The voice said, "I received confirmation that George is dead. But interestingly enough, he didn't die at the scene of the accident. He died in the hospital during surgery. That's a bit sloppy for my taste."

Shit. It was a bit sloppy, but it wasn't like he was going to climb down the embankment to check for a pulse. He would have probably ended up in the hospital himself. Thank the almighty, George Davis was dead. He certainly didn't need a mess, like if the jogger had survived.

Irwin clenched his fist. "I got the job done. That's what matters. When are you sending me the rest of my money?" He had planned to drive down to Mexico as soon as that money was in his deserving hands. He was ready, *yesterday*.

The voice said, "I'm a bit concerned. If you were that careless to leave the scene while he was still breathing, maybe you made a few other mistakes as well."

Irwin didn't like the sound of that. He assured him, "I took precautions. This won't come back on me."

Irwin realized he wasn't just convincing his employer, but also himself. He was sure he had done everything right. No license plates. He wore a hat, glasses, and gloves. He shook off the self-doubt. Irwin had been in this game for a long time and knew how to avoid the heat. This guy who insisted on being referred to as simply "employer" was a douche bag.

His employer said, "You'll get your money on Friday. I'll text the time and location to this phone an hour before. But know this, once you get that money, I don't know you, you don't know me. This exchange never happened. Are we clear?"

"Crystal."

"We have thirty-six hours until our business is concluded. Do me a favor and don't fuck this up before then."

Before Irwin could retort, the line went dead. He mumbled "asshole" under his breath before returning his attention to the football game.

CHAPTER FIVE

KENDALL

KENDALL STOOD WITH HER HEAD BOWED AS SHE STARED blankly at George's grave. She inhaled the scents of cut grass and damp earth as she tried to comprehend that she'd just witnessed her husband's body being lowered into the ground.

She twitched as she flashed back to standing over her parents' graves. She'd held her grandmother's hand as each person gave their condolences and pitied looks to her twelve-year-old self and her baby sister. Now she stood with Grandma and Janine, once again, as people gave the same condolences for her husband. Would everyone she loved be ripped from her?

Last week, she and George had been making plans for their fifth wedding anniversary. George said he wanted to go to an island so they could lay on the beach, sip cocktails, and make out like newlyweds. She had initially fought such a long trip because she was determined to make partner and didn't want to take the time off from work, but he'd finally worn her down, and she had agreed to two weeks in paradise. A promotion at the investment firm now seemed unimportant, frivolous.

She distinctly remembered thinking her life with George

was too good to be true. She usually liked being right, but not this time.

She'd met George at work. He was the handsome comptroller - brilliant, intelligent, and funny. They worked together for a year before he had asked her out. She was twenty-eight when they went on their first date, and on that night, she fell in love with him nearly instantly. His warm smile and sparkling blue eyes almost knocked her over after she'd opened the front door to her apartment.

When they lowered his casket into the ground, she stared in disbelief. Disbelief turned to anger, and she wanted to scream, "Stop! My husband is in there!" The world had begun to spin around her. If Janine hadn't been there, Kendall would've fallen to her knees.

She gazed to the right at her sister and grandmother. Janine gave her a sheepish grin. "Are you ready to head down to the reception hall for the wake?"

Was she ready to go to George's wake? Never. She inhaled and nodded her head. "As ready as I'll ever be."

Kendall's grandmother said, "You can have as much time as you need. Nobody will fault you for that. If you want to wait a few more minutes . . ."

"Thanks. Thank you for everything, Grandma."

Her grandmother tipped her head toward her. "You're very welcome, my sweet."

Kendall didn't know what she would've done if her grandmother hadn't made all the arrangements for George's funeral. She was too much of a wreck to do anything. Simple tasks like making a phone call or meeting with caterers seemed like monumental chores. She was lucky in so many ways to have her grandmother. After her parents had died, her grandmother hadn't hesitated to take her and Janine in and raise the two of them with love and a home-cooked meal every night. Grandma was the person she'd always turned to when she had a problem. She'd been Kendall's rock.

Grandma nudged Kendall's arm. "Who's that?"

Kendall stared ahead at the young detective and his muscled, middle-aged partner. "Oh, those are the detectives investigating the accident. They've been so kind."

One thing she'd been surprised to discover since George's death was how kind people could be—even strangers. There were flowers and cards from everyone she knew, and she had homemade meals for the next month all stacked up in her fridge. Detective Rogers had even been checking up on her daily to see how she was doing, providing updates on the case as new details emerged. He'd insisted she call him Marcus.

Janine said under her breath, "Kind on the eyes, that's for sure. Detective hot stuff can investigate me any day."

A smile crept over Kendall's face and she chuckled under her breath. She gazed at her younger sister, a senior at UC Berkeley studying computer science. Even in the worst circumstances, Janine could bring a smile to her face.

Kendall looped her arm through Janine's. "You are terrible, which is why I love you."

Kendall released her sister when the detectives approached.

Detective Rogers said, "Ms. Murphy, it was a beautiful ceremony. We are very sorry for your loss."

"Thank you. This is . . . this is my sister, Janine—you might remember her." She paused as she recalled standing over George's body and her sister bringing her out of the trance of disbelief. She continued, "And this is my grandmother."

Grandma extended her manicured hand with its lavender finger nails. "Grandma, just Grandma."

Detective Rogers shook her hand. "Thank you, ma'am, Grandma. I'm Detective Rogers and this is my partner, Detective Gates. It's nice to meet you. And yes, I remember Janine."

Janine batted her long eyelashes. "Hi."

Gates stepped in to shake Grandma's hand. "Condolences." He finished with a quick nod at Janine.

Detective Rogers continued, "We didn't see you at the wake, I wanted to make sure everything was okay?"

"We were taking our time, that's all," Grandma assured him.

Kendall perked up with an idea. Maybe they'd caught George's killer. "Why? Have you made progress on the case? Did you find who did this to George?"

"There have been some developments. I can't give any more details quite yet. As soon as I can, I will call you." Detective Rogers stared into Kendall's eyes. "We will find who did this to George. You have my word."

Gates gave Marcus what looked like a disapproving glare before pulling his phone from the inside of his dark-gray sport coat. Gates's eyes fell to the screen, and he said, "Excuse me, I have to take this." Gates stepped away from the small group.

From down the hill, Kendall spotted George's brother Howard heading toward them. Kendall was grateful that Howard and George didn't share much of a family resemblance. No, Howard had dark hair and eyes, with a doughy body—almost the complete opposite of George. George was like a golden God with honey-colored hair, bright-blue eyes, and a tall, muscled physique. She couldn't believe he'd never hold her in his arms again.

Howard reached the group. "We were getting worried about you. Is everything okay here?" He studied the detective. "Do I know you?"

Kendall didn't like the tone in Howard's voice. "We're fine. We were speaking to the detectives." She faced Marcus. "This is Howard, George's brother."

Marcus introduced himself.

Howard tipped his chin. "It would mean the world to us if

you could catch the animal who did this. I myself am devastated, but the news about George nearly killed our mother, and she's not well."

Kendall wasn't sure she bought the grieving-brother routine as heavy as he was putting it on. Howard and George weren't close. Not only were their physical appearances polar opposites, but their personalities as well. Rivals since childhood, they usually fought any time they were in the same room together. They only agreed to keep the peace for the sake of their ailing mother, and only saw each other once a year during the holidays upon his mother's insistence. Kendall never liked Howard much. Was he feigning sadness, hoping to be in George's will?

Gates rushed back to Marcus. "Something's come up. We need to go."

Marcus exchanged glances with Gates and nodded. "Again, condolences. Kendall, you have my number. If you need anything, day or night. Please call me. I'd like to help in any way I can."

Kendall gave her best attempt at a smile. "Thank you, Detective."

Janine waved flirtatiously. "Bye, Detective."

Marcus returned a brief smile before rushing after Gates.

Kendall playfully nudged her sister's arm. "C'mon. There's booze."

"You don't have to tell me twice."

Kendall led the march to what she imagined would be the worst party she would ever attend.

CHAPTER SIX

MARCUS

"Gates, wait up!" Marcus hollered.

Gates glanced over his shoulder at Marcus. He explained. "They found the car. Patrol and crime scene are there now. I figured you'd want to go right away. Am I right?"

Marcus grinned from ear to ear. He knew it. They'd found the car. They'd find the person who did this. He'd be able to keep his promise to Kendall.

The detectives approached the uniformed officer standing in front of the yellow crime scene tape, guarding the car that had hit George. Crime scene technicians were already on the scene taking photographs. Marcus stood in front of the vehicle and hunched down to inspect the badly damaged fender. There was no question. This was the car. He looked up at Gates. "What do you hear from the uniforms?"

Gates strutted over to Marcus. "So far nobody saw anything. But they just got here about twenty-five minutes ago. They haven't gone door-to-door. They decided to leave that to you and me. Lucky us. Like I haven't gotten enough exercise today roaming around the cemetery."

Marcus stood. "C'mon, a little exercise won't kill you."

"Say that to our friend George."

Marcus shook his head. "That's dark."

"Buddy, you'll find the need to have that kind of humor to survive this job."

Marcus supposed Gates was right, but the look of grief, sadness, and utter loss in Kendall's eyes was too fresh in his mind. He couldn't joke about the man's death. Marcus said, "Whatever. Let's start knockin' on doors."

"After you."

The door shut with a thud. Gates turned to Marcus. "We've been at this for almost an hour. We're over a mile from where the car was dropped. Buddy, I think we should call it."

Marcus chewed on his lower lip. Somebody had to have seen something. They couldn't give up now. He could feel they were too close to stop. Maybe they should come back tomorrow or the next day until somebody who saw something says they saw something? No, he was going to finish this today.

"Come on. Twenty more minutes and we can call it."

Gates shook his head at him. "I told you not to make promises. And don't think I don't see how you look at her. You need to knock that shit off. Nothing good will come from it. I'll give you twenty more minutes, and I'm done. Deal?"

He conceded. "Deal."

Shit. He needed to check himself. It wasn't that he was romantically interested in Kendall, he was just interested in knowing more about her. *Shit.* He did need to knock it off. He refocused on the case as they set off to find answers.

After the fifth person shut the door, Marcus felt the sweat trickle down his spine. He only had five more minutes, according to the agreement he made with Gates, and they still had nothing. Wait. They didn't have nothing, they had the car, but it could take days to process fingerprints and months for DNA results. He couldn't wait that long.

They approached a small, off-white home with a tidy lawn. Gates gave Marcus a look that said, *This is it.* Marcus knew the look. But he wasn't feeling defeated, not yet.

Marcus knocked on the door. A few moments later, a man in his forties with a goatee and wearing a white tank top that showed off heavily tattooed arms said, "Hey. What can I help you with?"

Gates puffed out his chest. "My name is Detective Gates, and this is my partner Detective Rogers. We're investigating a car accident. Wondering if maybe you saw anything strange Monday morning—three days ago? It would've been early. Did you see anything out of the ordinary? Maybe somebody walking around that you didn't recognize. Maybe a car you didn't recognize."

The man shifted his weight and put his hand on his hip. "There was this one dude. It was early, like 6:45 or 7 a.m. I was having my coffee and saw a guy. I didn't recognize him, and he kinda stood out. Older dude. Big. Maybe six-two. Hat. Glasses. Which I thought was odd because it was still dark out. Who wears sunglasses when it's dark?"

Marcus and Gates exchanged glances.

"Did you see where he was going?" Marcus asked.

The man stepped back and raised his arm and pointed across the street. "Yeah, over there. He walked toward a car parked across the street. It was a black car. Maybe an Acura or Honda. New. We don't have too many new cars in this neighborhood, if you haven't noticed."

Marcus wanted to jump across the threshold and give the man a hug, but by the looks of him, it probably would've started an altercation.

They continued to question the man about what he saw and recorded his statement, then they hurried down the driveway. When they hit the sidewalk, Gates faced Marcus. "You got lucky, my friend. You got a rabbit's foot in your pocket or something? Keep listening to that gut of yours, buddy. I'll call it in and get traffic footage coming in and out of the neighborhood. The perp probably called somebody to pick him up after the accident or to drop off a getaway car for him. If we find who owns the black car, we'll find the guy who killed George Davis."

Marcus said, "We're so damn close I can practically taste it. You call in the request for camera footage, and I'll see if patrol can pick us up; otherwise, we've got about a thirty-minute walk back."

Marcus was so pumped, he could have sprinted back and still had energy to spare.

Gates held his phone to his ear. "Good. Ain't no way I wanna walk all the way back. If I'm late for dinner, the wife gets pissed."

Back in their car, Gates and Marcus discussed their game plan for the next day. Gates glanced at the dashboard where his phone vibrated. He held up a finger. "Hold on." He picked up the phone. "Hey, what do you have for me?"

Marcus watched intently as Gates nodded.

"Thank you very much!" he exclaimed and hung up. "Heaven is smiling on us today. Were you praying earlier?"

"C'mon, man, what is it?"

"Buddy, we got a plate number and address of a 2017 black

Acura that left this neighborhood at 7:01 Monday morning."

Pounding his fists on the dash, Marcus said, "Fuck yeah. Excuse my language."

Gates laughed. "I'm guessing you want to check it out?"

"Drive!"

"If you had to deal with my wife, you wouldn't be so excited."

Adrenaline coursed through Marcus's legs and out his fingertips drumming the dash. He couldn't wait to see the look on the guy's face when they caught him. The owner of the car was either the perp, if a friend dropped off the perp's own car, or more likely, the owner of the car was a friend of the perp. If he was a friend, he would be an accessory after the fact; they'd make a deal to get him to roll on the perp. Easy. Score one for the good guys.

THEY APPROACHED THE ADDRESS GIVEN BY THEIR TECH guy. In the driveway was a man fitting the description made by the witness. A heavy-set older guy, maybe mid-fifties, loading a suitcase into the trunk of a black sedan.

Gates lowered his voice, narrowing his gaze out the window. "What are the odds this guy just happens to be taking a trip this week?"

A momentary loss for words at the fortunate break in the case, Marcus shook his head. "Not very likely. Let's do this." They exited the car and strutted over to the man.

Marcus called out, "Irwin Dratch?"

Irwin's body went rigid. "Yeah, who's asking?"

Marcus stood. "We're with the Ridgemont Police Department," he flashed his badge, "We'd like to ask you a few questions."

CHAPTER SEVEN

KENDALL

KENDALL CHOKED ON HER GLASS OF CHARDONNAY AND coughed, staring at the entrance of the trendy Aqua Restaurant. *No freaking way. Not today. Of all days. Why God? Why?*

From across the table, Janine lowered her head. "What? What's the matter?"

Kendall averted her gaze, down at the white tablecloth, as her heart pounded out of her chest. She'd had the bright idea to go to George's favorite restaurant after the wake for a drink, in honor of him, on the day they buried him. This was all her stupid idea, and now she was paying for it. "Oh nothing, just someone I used to work with, that I don't want to talk to."

Someone. Luke Abbington. Formally known as the love of her life before George. God, how she hoped he didn't see her. Did she have enough time to crawl under the table and hide out for the rest of her life—or until he left the restaurant? She was willing to do either if it meant she didn't have to talk to Luke.

"Kendall?"

Her stomach twisted at the sound of his voice. She took a gulp of wine before peering up at him. She was about two sips away from drunk, but she didn't care. Why had she thought going out was a good idea? Really, she should've remained home and drunk herself silly and fallen asleep on the couch as her family watched on with looks of pity in their eyes. The error in her logic was now quite clear. She said, "Uh, Luke. Hi."

Maybe if she just kept drinking, she'd become so ill she'd vomit, and then she'd have a legitimate excuse to leave the restaurant. The humiliation of puking in a restaurant was much better than having to face Luke. *Of all freaking days.* She didn't have the strength or the energy. She never would. She hadn't seen him in ten years. Why now? Why was life suddenly so Goddamn unfair? She wanted to scream, "Hey, universe, what gives?" but didn't.

Luke — mister tall, dark, and blah continued, "I wanted to come by and say how sorry I am. I heard about George. My condolences. Truly, I understand what you're going through. It's rough."

She'd forgotten that both George and Luke worked at Stickman Capital. Different departments, since George was the comptroller overseeing accounting practices at the firm, as opposed to Luke, a ruthless hedge fund manager. As far as she knew, they didn't even know each other. How did Luke know that she and George were married? Had the company posted something about his death and included her details? Probably.

She eked out, "Thanks," and averted her eyes once again, with the hopes that Luke would take the subtle cue and leave. He didn't. *Of course not.*

He said, "I just wanted to offer some help. It might be too soon for you, but I know that after my wife passed last year, I found a lot of comfort through a grief group a friend recommended. If you'd like, I can give you the information."

Kendall shook her head. Grief group? God that sounded like absolute torture. Grief group with Luke? A fate worse than death. She was more likely to scale the Golden Gate Bridge and jump from its highest point.

She glanced up at him and felt vomit inch up her throat. "I'll think about it. Thanks."

She covered her mouth with her hand, no longer in favor of the idea to barf, but the nerves in her stomach seemed to have other plans. Using all of her willpower, of which there wasn't much left in her reserve tank, she managed to prevent the bitter liquid from rising. She stared up at Luke, who had kept his eyes fixed on her. What the hell?

He said, "How about I give you my number and I can give you the details, or do you still have me in your phone?"

She absolutely did not have him in her phone anymore. No, she did not need a reminder of his existence. She lied, "Yeah, I think I still have it. Thanks."

He patted her on the shoulder and said, "Take care."

She nodded her head before finishing her much-needed glass of wine. Looking at Janine, she raised the empty goblet. "Get the waiter, I want another glass of wine."

Janine leaned forward, lowering her voice, "Are you sure?"

A bit slurred, slapping her palm on the table much to Janine's chagrin, Kendall demanded, "I've never been more sure. Another." It was finally time she found out what it was like to get blackout drunk. She hoped there would be memory loss.

CHAPTER EIGHT

IRWIN

"We have a problem." Irwin waited for a response for longer than he'd have liked. He repeated himself. "Did you hear me? I said we—have—a—problem." He slowed his speech to emphasize the extent of their issue.

His employer responded. "What do you mean *we* have a problem?"

Irwin didn't like the emphasis his employer put on the word *we*.

"There were two detectives at my house. They can't connect me to the car, but they can put me in the vicinity of where the car was parked. I told him I was in the neighborhood, searching for real estate prospects, and gave a whole spiel about making sure the neighborhood would be a good fit for me in my retirement, the quiet life and all." Irwin wasn't exactly lying about that. He did want a quiet life, but now he wanted it as far away from here as possible. Especially since he wasn't completely convinced the cops bought his story. Irwin continued, "I'll need the rest of my money tonight. I think it's too risky to meet tomorrow morning."

He wanted to get on his road trip to Mexico as soon as possible. He didn't like this kind of heat. He wanted to spend his retirement sipping margaritas, lying on a beach with some hot young thing, not in a cell bunking with a dude who had anger management issues.

His employer spat, "You're joking, right?"

Irwin stiffened, clenching his fist. "I am not joking. I think it's best. I get the money tonight, I get out of town, and this whole thing goes away."

"You're insane if you think I'll meet with you tonight. They could be watching you right now. You shouldn't even be calling me. What were you thinking? I knew you were a mistake. Now here you are, fucking things up. I should have gone with my instincts."

Irwin barely refrained from throwing the phone across his living room. His plan was falling apart, and this asshole was getting on his last fucking nerve. He needed that money to go to Mexico, as part of his plan. Should he forgo the money at this point? Was that even possible? He shook his head and grumbled, "Look, let's give it a couple of days, buy a little time for this to blow over. I'll give you a call, and we'll make a plan." He felt good about being in control, rational. This was what he needed. This wasn't the time to get nervous. Nervous turned into sloppy. He would stay the course.

"In a few days? You think this will all blow over in a few days? You've gotta be kidding. You know, I'm starting to think you didn't earn your fee. You're supposed to make it look like an accident, with no suspicion on you or me, and now you've gone and fucked it all up. First, he didn't die at the scene, and now, detectives are sniffing around. I'm starting to believe you didn't fulfill your contract, and that maybe, this is the end of our relationship."

Fury coursed through Irwin's veins. "You listen to me. You will pay me for services rendered, or else this could get very unpleasant for you." Did this guy forget who he was talking to? He'd been a contract killer since the asshole was in diapers. He would get paid one way or another.

His employer said, "I'll be in touch." And then the line went dead.

Irwin threw his cell phone down on the sofa and paced around the room. That asshole was not going to stiff him on this job. He performed the services.

All the guy needed to do was give him his money and he would be on his way. Irwin needed that money; it was part of his retirement package. He needed to crunch his numbers again to see if he could do without this additional funding. He grabbed a cigarette and lit it before taking a long drag. He exhaled a cloud of smoke. Mexico was calling his name. He could leave now and not look back. That would be the smart thing to do, but self-respect refused to let that jerk stiff him on the payment. He would get his money, or his revenge. It would be the asshole's choice which.

CHAPTER NINE

MARCUS

Marcus jumped up from his seat and hunched over the surveillance technician's shoulder, who was currently scanning through the traffic footage on the monitor. "Go back."

Ronnie, a thirty-something hipster with dark-framed glasses, scrolled across his mousepad to the prior sixty seconds.

Marcus tapped on the desk. "No, further back, maybe to ninety seconds."

The tech continued to roll back the footage. Marcus's eyes brightened. "Yeah, there." He pointed at the screen. "Now start and freeze on the driver's face."

"Front or side view?" Ronnie asked.

"Do you have a front view?"

"There's a camera across from this one that will likely have the front view."

"Let's start with the side and then the front."

"You got it, boss."

Ronnie grabbed the mouse and clicked, cropping the profile view of the driver, enlarging it, and then enhancing it for a clearer picture of the suspect.

Marcus stared at the screen in amazement. The driver wore

a black baseball cap, dark Ray-Ban style sunglasses, and sported a bushy mustache. His large hands were hidden beneath black leather gloves that clutched the steering wheel of the Lincoln Town Car as he eased through the traffic light onto a city street near where they'd found the car.

They had him. That man was George Davis's killer, and Marcus was going to take him down. It would be difficult to discern the facial features, but the driver's head in relation to the vehicle would give them an approximate height and weight.

If he were to speculate, the murderer was a tall, burly man, quite like their new friend Irwin Dratch. Dratch didn't have a mustache, but that was an easy shave. *Shoot.* Dratch wasn't an accessory to the act, he was the driver. They wouldn't be able to identify him based on the photo, but now they knew to put a patrol car on him. "Can you print that for me?"

"No problem."

Ronnie tapped his slender fingers on the mouse and waited for the printer across the room to spit out the photo.

Marcus grabbed it off the machine.

Ronnie said, "I'll work on the other camera. You want to wait, or do you want me to call when I've got it?"

"Go ahead and give me a call. Also, next, can you work on the cameras around where the car was stolen?"

"You got it."

Marcus headed back to the office area where he'd started a board to track all the evidence they'd collected for George Davis's case. He tacked up the photo of their prime suspect and stood back, satisfyingly crossing his arms. He knew Dratch was crooked. He hadn't believed his real estate story for a second. Who would move from a nice quiet neighborhood, like where Dratch lived, to some shady part of town for their retirement? Highly unlikely. His demeanor was off too. Most people were nervous around police, but Dratch, he was a bit too smooth.

Dratch was definitely responsible for the hit-and-run—that much Marcus was convinced of. But what they didn't know was why he'd stolen the old car. What else was he doing that morning where he needed a stolen car to do it? Who *was* Irwin Dratch?

"They told me I could find you in here," came a familiar female voice from behind.

Marcus glanced over his shoulder and did a double take. It was Kendall Murphy. A combination of desperation and defeat painted her delicate face. It was clear she hadn't been getting much sleep. Her emerald-green eyes were outlined by dark circles. Her skin was pale, making the freckles across the bridge of her nose more prominent. Despite those facts, she was a beautiful woman. He wished he'd seen what she looked like before her husband's death extinguished the light in her eyes. *Shit, Marcus. Stop it. She's the vic's widow.* He walked toward her, casually stepping away from the board of evidence, hoping she wouldn't see. Who in their right mind would send her back here? "Yes, Kendall, how are you doing? What can I help you with?"

She said, "Well, they told me I could find you here . . ." Her attention shifted to the board behind Marcus.

Shit. He watched as her eyes followed left and right and up and down. She stopped at the suspect's photo. "Is that him? Is that the person who did this to George?" Tears formed in the corners of her eyes.

He wanted to comfort her, but also didn't want to cross the line. He knew better and avoided any and all physical contact with female coworkers, suspects, and family members of victims. The department had been clear on the new policy. He said, "We think so." He raised his hand toward her arm, not touching her, but in an effort to guide her gaze away from the board and toward his desk.

"Do you have a name?"

He lowered his arm. "Not yet. He'll be difficult to identify since most of his features are distorted by the hat, glasses, and mustache. We do have some leads and persons of interest we're talking to. However, at this time we don't have enough evidence to arrest anyone. But believe me, Kendall, we will get him. It just may take a little bit longer than we thought."

He watched as her face fell.

She stared at the floor for a few moments before she jerked her head up and fixed her eyes on him. "Is there anything I can do to help? I read the news. I know the city is over budget. I have all kinds of time. I'm on leave from work, and they won't let me come back. I need to keep busy or I'll go crazy. Please. I have nothing to do, other than sitting in my house eating casseroles and having friends and neighbors ask me how I'm doing. How am I doing? I'm terrible, thanks for asking. My husband died. My world was blown apart. I need to do something. I can't sit around and do nothing. Please, Detective, let me help bring justice for my husband. I'll do anything. I'll get coffee, hand out flyers. Anything. Really."

For the first time since he met Kendall Murphy, he saw a tiny spark of hope behind her grief.

"Unfortunately, I'm not sure how much you can do at this point, but if you have any questions about the case, I'll answer them the best I can and . . ." He stopped when he realized she was no longer paying attention to him; rather, she was focused on the photograph of the suspect.

Kendall turned her head in slow motion, her auburn hair swinging across her face. She tucked the loose strands behind an ear, then faced him with wide eyes. "You said you couldn't identify him because of the hat, glasses, and frankly, the horrible mustache. Is that right?"

"Yes, that's true, unfortunately, but—"

"What about the ears?"

Marcus cocked his head. "What do you mean?"

"A while back I read an article about how scientists have proven that ears are as unique as a fingerprint. You can make a positive identification by comparing the ears in the photo to another person's ear. If there's a match, you get your guy—it's just like comparing fingerprints."

Marcus was stunned. "Are you serious?"

"Yeah, look." She tapped on her smartphone, searching for the information, and then handed it to Marcus.

He read the article. How had his department not utilized this new software and technique? He knew the answer. It was always the same answer. It wasn't in the budget. He tried to fight his anger at how close they had come to not being able to identify their suspect. He handed Kendall back her phone. "Looks like you were able to help after all. I need to go down to tech right now and get the ears enhanced. You'll have to excuse me."

"Can I come with you?" she pleaded.

"I'm sorry, only department personnel allowed down in the cave. I'll call you as soon as we find out something, okay?"

She nodded.

Marcus said goodbye and texted Gates, before grabbing the photo from the wall and rushing down the flight of stairs to 'the cave,' what they called the video surveillance room.

When he entered the room, Ronnie, surrounded by half a dozen monitors, was hunched over, studying footage from the traffic cams. He looked over his shoulder at the detective. "Hey man, what's up?"

He placed the photograph on the tech's desk. "Any way to enhance this to get really good detail on the ears?"

Ronnie pushed his glasses up the bridge of his nose. "Probably. I'll give it my best shot."

Ronnie closed out of the current screen and opened up the still shot of the suspect's profile he'd worked on earlier. Marcus hovered behind him as he worked, waiting, unable to remain still.

After a few minutes, Marcus placed both hands on top of the desk, staring intently at the screen. "You got it. Awesome. It should be enough to get a match, right?"

"On the ears? Probably. I was at a conference a few months ago where they discussed identification using ears. Is that what you're trying to do? I've never seen it used here before. We don't have the software, but I'm pretty sure there are other departments who do. I can make a few calls to some of my colleagues."

Marcus slapped Ronnie on the shoulder. "Yes, please, and thank you."

Marcus paced back and forth in the cave as Ronnie called around for the software. The small space was suffocating and had a dank smell. How did Ronnie stand it down here all day? Would the ear match actually work?

Twenty minutes later and too many discouraging head shakes, Ronnie gave him a thumbs up. Marcus had to hold himself back from giving the man a hug. "Thank you!"

Before Marcus could exit, the door popped open and Gates stood in the doorway. "Got your message. What's going on? What did you find? It better be good, considering it's Saturday, and I was having a lovely day lounging around and watching football."

Marcus stepped forward and handed him the original, uncropped photo. He smirked. "Who does that look like to you?"

Gates grabbed the picture and inspected it. "Holy shit. Is that the driver of the Lincoln?"

"Yep. Our pal here obtained the traffic footage from nearby stoplights, a much better visual than we got from the home surveillance videos. He was able to zoom in and then enhance them to get a good picture of the driver."

Gates frowned. "I mean, it looks like Irwin Dratch, I'll give you that. Actually, I'd probably bet some coin on it, but buddy—the eyes, the forehead, the mouth, they're all covered. There's no way to get a positive ID from that."

Marcus lifted his index finger in the air. "Exactly what I thought." Marcus handed him the blown-up picture of the ear. "Until . . ."

Gates shook his head. "I don't follow. What is this?"

"It's an ear. And guess what? You can get an ID based on an ear. They're as unique as a fingerprint."

"Come again?"

Marcus went on to explain the visit from Kendall Murphy and the revelation about ear identification. He showed him the articles and let Ronnie explain that other departments had been doing it for a little while now, which means they had access to the technology. All they needed was a match.

Gates's hazel eyes widened. "Well, holy shit. Let's go get the son-of-a-bitch."

"Shouldn't we get a warrant first?" Marcus asked.

Gates held up the photo of the enhanced picture of the ear. "No time. If he opens his door, and his ear looks anything like this, we have probable cause, plus he has no alibi. Even if it's not enough to hold him for longer than forty-eight hours, it'll be enough time for us to get the ear match confirmed in order to officially charge him. Let's go."

Marcus and Gates thanked Ronnie and hurried out of the cave and upstairs to their desks. Marcus stopped cold when he saw Kendall standing in front of the board. "Did you find anything?" she asked.

Marcus explained, "We were able to enhance the picture.

We're on our way now to talk to a person of interest. It's best if you go home. I promise I'll call you with an update."

Gates eyed Kendall and then Marcus.

"We really need to go, now," Gates reminded him.

Marcus nodded.

He faced Kendall. "I'm really sorry. I'll call you as soon as I have news, I promise."

Her blank stare returned. "Okay."

Marcus tried to ignore the distraught look on Kendall's face. He couldn't worry about her right now; he needed to do his job. Marcus grabbed his jacket and waved as he and Gates rushed out of the station.

CHAPTER TEN

MARCUS

Marcus threw his phone on the dashboard. "Backup is on the way." Adrenaline soaring, he could run a marathon with the amount of energy pulsing through his body.

He couldn't wait to watch as the officers cuffed the animal that killed George Davis. Who hits a guy on the side of the road and doesn't stop to call for help? A real cretin, that's who. Scum like that didn't deserve to walk around free.

Gates remained focused on the road. "We got lucky. However, I do have to admit your tireless efforts are likely the real reason we're able to catch this guy. How many hours have you worked on this case in the last five days? Maybe you not having a life isn't such a bad thing after all. That approach is good for the department and for catching bad guys, but not so great for you, buddy. I still think you need to be careful."

Marcus appreciated his partner's concern, but his priority was fighting for those who have no one else to speak for them. He had to focus on his career. His personal life could wait. Besides, he had plans. After the George Davis investigation was closed, he was going to approach the Lieutenant about working on his brother's case. He'd earned it.

Marcus shrugged. "I don't know. I slept a few nights." And when he said a few nights, he meant he'd slept for a few hours of those few nights. He'd catch up on his sleep after Irwin Dratch was in jail.

A niggling in his gut still had him questioning why Irwin Dratch had been out driving that morning. And why had he stolen a car? And who had dropped off his getaway car? What other criminal activity was he involved in?

"What do you suppose Dratch was doing that morning when he hit George Davis? He doesn't have an alibi, and he was driving a stolen car."

Gates looked over at Marcus. "That's a good question. The guy's got a clean sheet, but that doesn't mean he's a choir boy either. It's a bit peculiar, I'll give you that, buddy."

Dratch was definitely up to something, but what? Marcus said, "You think there's any chance Dratch didn't know he'd hit George Davis that morning?"

Gates sighed. "It was dark and early. If he was under the influence, which we will never be able to prove at this point, I think a good lawyer could argue he didn't know he hit a person. George's body was found down an embankment. So he could have thought he'd hit an animal. You know, if he looked at the road, there was probably no sign of George. But I think the son-of-a-bitch knew. Why else would he drop off a car and pick up another?" Gates cocked his head to the right. "But you know, if he was up to something sketchy that morning, he could've been in a pretty big hurry and hadn't realized he'd hit George until later."

Marcus thought back and shook his head. "No. George's hands, ankles, and clothing were covered in reflectors. Dratch had to have seen him, unless he didn't have his headlights on. But we know that they were, based on the neighborhood surveillance videos, which means he had to have seen George."

"Buddy, I agree. But don't be surprised if his defense lawyer comes up with some BS story about how he didn't know it and how he's an upstanding citizen who feels just terrible for George and the family. I've seen it before."

It was exactly what Marcus was afraid of. He didn't want Dratch to walk. He wanted justice for George Davis and Kendall. He wouldn't accept some lame misdemeanor hit-and-run charge with a minuscule fine. No, this was felony hit-and-run, vehicle manslaughter, and felony grand theft auto. He would not let Dratch go free, if it was the last thing he did.

Gates eased up in front of Irwin Dratch's house and turned off the engine. Marcus commented, "Car is in the driveway. He hasn't fled, yet, unless, of course, he stole another car."

"I think that would be too risky. It'd look damn suspicious if he ran."

Marcus agreed, but wondered why Dratch hadn't run. Sure, he'd look suspicious, but he'd also have gotten away. What if for some reason he wasn't worried about being caught? Another cocky criminal? Maybe. Dratch had no record. What else was he doing that morning? Nobody steals a car to drive it around at six o'clock in the morning without a purpose. Would they ever really know what he'd done? Marcus supposed that if they booked him on the charges related to George's death, it might not matter.

Gates glanced in the mirror. "All right, backup's here. It's time to rock 'n' roll."

Gates and Marcus jogged down the path to Dratch's front porch. Marcus banged his fist on the door. His heart pumped, coursing blood through his veins. This was it. They were going to take him down.

The door creaked open. Irwin Dratch eyed both the detectives before glancing past them at the patrol cars. He refocused on Marcus. "What can I help you with detective?"

Gates held up the photo of the ear. Marcus inspected the right side of Irwin's head. He studied Dratch's ear and gave Gates a nod. Marcus looked directly into Irwin Dratch's eyes. "Please step out of the house."

A smirk appeared on Dratch's face as he stepped out onto the porch.

Marcus continued, "Irwin Dratch, you're under arrest for felony hit-and-run of George Davis on November 4, 2019. In addition, you have charges relating to vehicular manslaughter and grand theft auto."

As Marcus read him his rights, Irwin extended his hands out in front of him, as if asking for the handcuffs. *He's too calm*, Marcus thought. It was as if he were expecting the arrest and didn't care. It unnerved Marcus.

The handcuffs clicked shut.

Dratch stared into Marcus's eyes. "Lawyer."

Marcus's heart dropped. Gates told the patrol officers to take Dratch back to the station.

With Dratch out of earshot, Marcus turned to Gates with fury in his eyes. "What the hell was that?"

Gates shook his head. "I don't know. This keeps getting weirder and weirder."

Marcus wanted to punch something. This was not how it was supposed to go. Irwin Dratch was no innocent bystander who didn't notice he'd hit another human being on the side of the road. Nobody was that calm or that cocky, unless they were hiding something or knew something the police didn't. At that moment, Marcus vowed that he wouldn't stop investigating until he found out exactly what Irwin Dratch was up to the morning of George Davis's death.

CHAPTER ELEVEN

KENDALL

Kendall sipped rich, black coffee while she watched her sister at the stove, laboring over a frying pan. Sadness filled her as she recalled the last person she had seen standing at the range—George.

Each morning he'd insisted she eat breakfast or at least bring one of his green smoothies with her to work. On the weekends, he'd fry up a special egg dish with seasonal veggies, or if it were a special occasion, banana pancakes or French toast with real maple syrup.

She realized she missed the sound of the blender in the morning. It used to irritate her as she readied for work, but now the kitchen was far too quiet. She still hadn't fully comprehended that he was never coming back, as if he were simply away on one of his business trips, like he did from time to time.

Several times a day, she'd expect that he would just walk in, as if nothing had ever happened and that the last week had been a bizarre and awful nightmare. They'd hug and kiss and make their way upstairs.

Her grandmother and sister and friends made sure that she hadn't been alone much over the last week, but she had finally convinced her grandmother to give her a little bit of space. Still, Kendall had been pleased when Janine decided to come by the night before and stay over to visit. She was the only one who didn't treat Kendall like she was a raw egg about to crack. She wasn't. Not really. Sure, she wept rather regularly, but no amount of company would stop that. She was heartbroken. There was no cure, and the only treatment was time.

Janine set down the plate with a thud. "Eggs à la Janine."

Kendall stared at the plate of scrambled eggs with feta cheese and chopped green onions sprinkled on top. "Thank you. It looks great. When did you learn how to cook?"

Janine slid into her seat, across from Kendall, and flipped her long auburn hair to the left. "I've been cooking for Grandma. She's been a little forgetful lately."

Kendall set down her fork. "What do you mean?"

"We don't need to discuss this now."

"Spill."

"I was going to bring it up earlier, but then . . . George." Janine lowered her gaze. "Really, we don't need to do this now."

Kendall sunk into her chair. She couldn't lose Grandma. She didn't think she'd survive that too. "It's fine. Please tell me, Janine."

"Okay. Grandma's been forgetting things, so we took her to the doctor. He thinks it's the early signs of dementia."

"But she planned the whole funeral and wake. She seemed completely normal. I didn't notice anything off." Kendall paused. "But then again, I wasn't exactly in a place to evaluate anyone's mental state."

"The doctor said she can have days and days with no symptoms—in the beginning. She's fine for now, but I wanted you to know. The doctor warned that we should be considering the future and figure out what that looks like for Grandma while she's still fairly high-functioning."

The two of them ate without speaking for a minute. Kendall didn't know what to make of this. Grandma, Janine, and a few close friends were all the family she had left.

Janine continued, "I should reiterate, she's high functioning now and she hasn't been in danger. Actually, Grandma and I were talking, and we were thinking maybe if you wanted—no pressure— I could stay here for a little while. Maybe until the school year is out."

The idea shocked Kendall. "But it's so far from school. You'd be in traffic for at least an hour each way. Not to mention, what if Grandma needs you? She's fine now, but what if there is a rapid decline? No, I don't think so. We can't leave her alone."

"Well actually, she and Mary were talking about moving into one of those swanky retirement communities. She was planning to wait until I was done with school, but since . . . Grandma has already talked to Mary about moving in sooner. She's excited about it and she'll have twenty-four-hour access to medical services."

Kendall hadn't realized how much she had missed in her grandmother's life. Dementia. Moving into a retirement community with her best friend? George's accident gave Kendall a reason, an excuse to be out of the loop, but what about before that? Had she been so focused on her career and starting her own family with George that she'd been neglecting her existing family? All two of them. Where were her priorities? That stopped now. Family first. Stock market be damned.

Janine tilted her head at her sister. From time to time, it startled her how much her sister looked like a younger version of herself.

Kendall shut her eyes and reopened them. "I'll *be* fine. Really. I need to deal with my new reality, right? I'm going to be alone for a long while." She stopped pleading her case as her eyes began to well with tears. Life was harder when she was alone, but delaying the adjustment to living alone wouldn't do her any good. Or would it?

"Well, the offer stands. I'm totally okay with it. There's only another month before the semester is over. And then one more semester and I'm a graduate! I mean it's not that much time at all, the commute is not the end of the world. I'm into so many podcasts right now, the drive will fly by. But no pressure. I understand if you'd rather be here by yourself. But if you change your mind, I'll be here in a flash."

Kendall mumbled, "Thank you."

"Have you decided what you'll do with George's things?"

Her heart stopped. His things. Their house. Their things. It was too much to think about.

She had spaced out longer than she realized when her sister said, "Kendall?"

"I don't know. I haven't really thought about it. I mean, it's not urgent, right?"

"No, of course not. I just wondered if maybe you wanted my help?"

"You really have been conspiring with Grandma, haven't you?"

Janine shrank into her shoulders. "Guilty."

Kendall attempted a smile but was sure she'd failed. "I appreciate it. I think when I'm ready to do any of those things, I'll let you know. I'm not ready yet . . ." her voice trailed off.

Her nose tingled as the tears returned, and she buried her face in her hands, sobbing quietly.

Kendall raised her head and wiped the tears with the back of her hand—she was a mess. "I'm sorry. One minute I'm okay and can have a normal conversation, and then the next, I'm not. It comes without warning like a cruel surprise." Would she ever go a day without crying? It didn't seem likely.

"You don't have to apologize. Have you considered what

your friend recommended, you know, to attend a grief group? Maybe that will help. Maybe it'll help to talk about it or be around other people who have gone through what you've been through."

"Friend? What friend?"

"At the restaurant. The super-hot guy that came up to our table. You know, the one with the dark hair and the yummy five o'clock shadow. He's a bit old for me, but damn. He fine. *That* friend. I think you said he was a coworker?"

The nerves in her stomach made her believe she'd be sick. *Right. Luke Abbington.* Not her friend. But her sister didn't know that. The only person who'd known what had happened was her best friend, Beth. The truth was, Kendall had only been a momentary blip in Luke's life, but he was years of heartache in hers.

She said, "Oh, I don't know. Maybe." She was open to the idea of attending a group for grieving widows, but sure as the sky was blue, it wouldn't be a group that included Luke, that's for damn sure.

Janine offered. "I can call him to get the information for you, if you'd like."

She sniffled. "Oh, I don't actually have his phone number. I only said I did to make him go away."

Janine's brows furrowed. "Well played."

Kendall used her napkin to finish wiping her eyes and her cheeks. She chuckled halfheartedly. "Thanks." She began to reconsider her sister's offer to move in. Janine was the only thing that seemed to be able to make her smile. Maybe Kendall was wrong. Maybe having her sister around would make her remember there was a reason to go on and to know that smiling was possible. Her thoughts were interrupted by the sound of the doorbell.

Janine jumped up from the table. "Detective Hottie is here." She flipped her hair and winked. "How do I look?"

Kendall suppressed a smile as she shook her head. When had Janine become so boy crazy?

Detective Rogers sat across the kitchen table from Janine and Kendall, sipping the freshly brewed coffee Janine had made. He set down the red mug and fixed his light blue eyes on Kendall. "Now, why I'm here. I wanted to update you on the current status of the investigation —"

Kendall interrupted. Her face was serious and her eyes were wide. "Did you catch him? Did the ear recognition work?"

Marcus nodded. "Yes, we'll be able to confirm his identity based on the ear." He glanced over at Janine. "I don't know if your sister told you, but she was the one who told us about ear identification, and that's how we were able to apprehend the man responsible for George's accident."

Janine said, "Yes, she mentioned it. Who would've thought? I feel like if this got out, criminals around the world would know they'd need more than a baseball cap to disguise themselves. You may find a new breed of criminals running around, wearing those dorky hiking hats to cover their whole face, neck, and ears."

Marcus snickered. "I certainly hope not, but some are smart enough to do so."

"Who is this guy? Who is the man that killed my husband? What's his name? Tell me everything about him," Kendall demanded.

Marcus shifted in his chair. "The person we believe to be the driver is a man named Irwin Dratch. He's fifty-five years old and from Concord. Not only was he the driver, but we also believe he stole the vehicle that hit your husband. He will be charged with felony hit-and-run, vehicular manslaughter, and felony grand theft auto."

Janine's eyes lit up. "So, this guy will go away for a long time, right?"

Marcus sat back. "We hope so. But I want to prepare you for what *could* happen. We arrested him yesterday, and he requested a lawyer immediately. At this point, he is refusing to cooperate in any way with us. He'll only talk to his lawyer. There's a bail hearing scheduled for Monday. It's possible he'll get out of jail on bail and remain free until the trial. Assuming there is a trial. The district attorney wants to charge him with all of the offenses and is requesting the longest sentence applicable due to the severity of the crime. However, his conviction of the crime may not be as straightforward as we originally hoped."

"What do you mean?" Kendall asked.

"There's still some evidence that we're evaluating and analyzing. As of now, he could have a defense strategy indicating he didn't know that he had hit your husband and that's why he didn't stop. He could also say that a friend loaned him the car, and he didn't know that it was stolen. And if for some reason they can convince a jury or a judge of this, or create reasonable doubt, he could walk on all charges."

Kendall slammed her hands down on the table and stood up. "You're fucking kidding me. You have the guy, but you think he may go free? It doesn't make any sense."

Janine put her arm around Kendall in an attempt to calm her and for her to sit back down. "Come on, sis, let's finish listening to what Detective Rogers has to say, okay?"

Kendall righted the chair and sat, fuming. "Okay. Tell us what else."

"We're fairly confident we'll be able to prosecute. However, I wanted to prepare you for the chance of the case going sideways. It's not a slam dunk. However, we're hoping the evidence we're analyzing will allow us to put together a good enough case to prosecute. I think a reasonable judge and a reasonable jury would see that Irwin Dratch is responsible and should be found guilty of all charges. In the coming weeks and months, we'll prepare for the trial, unless he pleads out."

"Pleads out?"

Marcus leaned forward and placed his hands on the table. "The district attorney may choose to offer him a deal, to avoid the expense of a trial. Right now, he's facing a maximum of twelve to fifteen years. If he pleads guilty, that sentence could be reduced to two to five years. If he has a good lawyer, maybe even less time, or he could be cleared of all charges if brought to trial. Between you and me, my gut says this case is likely to go to trial. If that happens, it could be rough on you and your family because these things can drag on for quite some time, possibly years. But we'll do everything in our power to not let that happen. In my conversations with the district attorney, they're hoping for a speedy trial."

Kendall's brows lifted. "Years?"

Marcus frowned. "We'll try to not let that happen. We have a strong case, and we're working on strengthening it further. I'm telling you all of this because often the family attends the trial, which can help the prosecution. If that is something you would be up to when the time comes. I haven't seen George's brother, Howard, or his mother since the funeral. Are they local?"

Kendall shook her head. "No, they live in Bakersfield. I haven't seen or heard from them since the funeral either. Their father passed a few years ago. Howard is his mother's caretaker, and she's quite ill with cancer. I'm not sure how she's doing. I haven't checked in. I should." Kendall spaced out. She should call her mother-in-law. George would have liked that.

"Kendall?" Detective Rogers asked.

She shook her head. "Sorry. I don't think they will be able to attend in her condition."

Kendall was reminded of how small both George's family and her family are. The two of them had hoped to change that. They recently planned their anniversary trip, which would have been their first baby-making mission. George wanted three kids. She thought he was nuts to want that many children, but now she wished they'd had a whole house full of kids. She'd give up anything to have him back.

"Very well. Then I'll make sure you're updated every step of the way. Family doesn't typically attend the arraignment, but you're welcome to. It's tomorrow."

Kendall turned to her sister. "Do you think I should go?" Kendall wasn't sure how she felt about seeing the man who killed her husband. It was one thing to see him in a photo, but quite another to see him in person. Would she fly off into a rage? Break down and cry and scream at him that he'd stolen her future?

"If you want to, I could go with you. I have school but I don't have any tests or anything I can't miss."

Kendall said, "I'd like to go to the arraignment."

Marcus said, "Then I'll leave you the details."

She stared at the detective, with more resolve. There was no way she'd miss the opportunity to look into the eyes of the man who killed her husband. Irwin Dratch needed to see her, see what he'd done, who George left behind.

MONDAY MORNING, KENDALL CLUTCHED HER SISTER'S ARM as she watched the man accused of killing her husband enter the courtroom. He didn't look remorseful as his lawyer pleaded that, "Irwin Dratch was a law-abiding citizen with no record" and that he'd simply, "made a terrible mistake" in thinking he'd hit an animal and not a person. The lawyer pleaded that if Dratch had known, he of course would've stopped and offered help.

As the judge set Irwin's bail to the amount his lawyer requested, hatred sprinted through Kendall. An evil smirk formed on Irwin Dratch's face.

Free on bail!

The sound of the gavel made her jump.

"Kendall, are you okay?" whispered Janine.

She shook her head. "Free on bail."

"C'mon, let's go."

Janine led her out of the courtroom. The sisters were greeted in the lobby by Detectives Rogers and Gates. Detective Rogers said, "I'm sorry it went this way, but unfortunately, it's what we expected."

Expected? Detective Rogers had made it sound like bail was a possibility, but not exactly expected. Kendall stared at the floor and crossed her arms. "It doesn't make sense that someone could take a life and then be allowed to go about his own life."

Marcus placed his hand on her shoulder. "Kendall, we'll get him at trial."

She looked up at him. "It's going to trial?"

Detective Gates stepped forward, and Marcus let his hand drop. Detective Gates said, "We think so, since his lawyer is pleading his innocence. But as the trial progresses, Irwin Dratch could still have a chance for a plea deal, cutting the trial short. We'll keep you apprised of the progress. The next step is for Detective Rogers and me to work with the DA to build the best possible case against Dratch. We want him to go away for a long time."

Marcus interjected, "We'll do our best to make sure that happens."

"But you can't be sure." Kendall's heart pounded. "What do I do now?"

Detective Gates said, "There's not a lot you can do for now. As we mentioned, it could be anywhere from a few weeks up to six months, before the preliminary hearing."

Kendall's eyes darted from detective to detective. "Six months?"

Detective Rogers said, "I'll be in touch. Call me anytime, okay?"

Kendall watched as Detective Gates gave Marcus a stern look. "Okay."

Janine said, "C'mon sis, let's get out of here. Ice cream? My treat."

Her husband's killer was walking free, and Janine thought ice cream would help? She was twenty-two; she had no idea what it was like to have her world slip away. When she and her sister lost their parents, Janine was only a baby, but Kendall remembered the day like it were yesterday. She had survived that, and hopefully she'd survive this too. "All right. Let's get out of here."

Kendall nodded to the detectives and headed out of the courthouse. Ice cream wouldn't help, but it couldn't hurt either.

CHAPTER TWELVE

SIX MONTHS LATER, KENDALL

Kendall wrapped her arms around her baby sister. "I'm so proud of you, Janine!" Kendall stepped back, in awe of her sister. She wished their parents could have been there to see how wonderful Janine had turned out. A brilliant computer scientist with love, wit, and confidence to spare. Her auburn hair flowing in the breeze, Janine beamed as she posed in her black cap and gown in front of UC Berkeley's Sather Gate. She couldn't believe Janine was a college graduate. She felt the welling of tears.

They stopped abruptly with a plea from Janine. "Oh, come on! You aren't getting mushy on me, are you?"

Grandma wrapped an arm around Janine, and said, "You're all grown up now. I remember when you were just a toddler running around ripping doilies off my end tables."

Kendall chortled. "I nearly forgot! She'd put them on her head—swearing it was her princess crown—and then she'd dance around the living room." The three erupted into laughter.

"Yes. I was adorable, wasn't I? Can we finish this trip down memory lane at the restaurant, now that we've taken," Janine glanced at Kendall's phone in her hands, "what? Four, five *thou-*

sand pictures? I want my first cocktail as a college graduate, and also, I'm famished." She rubbed her stomach. "Wasn't that ceremony the longest ever, or what?"

Kendall said, "You don't have to ask me twice. Let's go."

The three strolled leisurely down Telegraph Avenue, smiling in the sunshine, not bothered by the stench of garbage that the street was famous for.

Kendall almost forgot that six months ago her world had been turned upside down. *What's the saying? Oh, right. "Almost" doesn't count.* Too distracted by her thoughts, she stumbled into someone amongst the sea of people on the sidewalk. She stopped and stepped back. "I'm so . . . sorry." Her heart sank. *No.*

Luke grinned. "Kendall, what are the odds of running into you again? You're looking"—he studied Kendall—"*well,* by the way." His eyes slid over to Grandma and Janine. "Is this little Janine? And you must be her grandmother."

What the hell was he doing? How did he remember Janine's name and who Grandma was? Sure, they'd spent hours upon hours talking, and Kendall had, of course, always rambled on about her little sister and grandma, but she was pretty sure she'd meant nothing to him and that he'd never really paid attention to anything she'd ever said. So why, ten years later, did he still remember? Maybe he just had a good memory. Kendall tipped her head to the side, examining his irritatingly handsome appearance, as if peering into his mind. He *was* one of the most intelligent men she'd ever known. Kendall shook the ridiculous, intrusive thought away.

Janine glanced at Kendall. "Yes, I'm Janine, Kendall's sister, and this is our Grandma."

Grandma eyed Kendall before focusing on Luke. "Why yes, I don't believe we've met."

Luke placed his hand over his chest and dipped his head.

"I'm so sorry. Of course not. I'm Luke Abbington. Kendall and I used to work together. It's been a while, hasn't it?" he paused. "We ran into one another some months back. Kendall, how long has it been since we worked together?"

Not long enough. "I think ten, going on eleven years? A while for sure. Also . . ." She glanced at Grandma and Janine. "Luke worked at the same company as George."

Luke's overly confident smile seemed to fade, and he cupped his hands together. "Yes, I currently work at Stickman Capital. I didn't know George, but we were at the same company at the same time. Again, I'm sorry for your loss." He rested a hand on Kendall's lower arm, standing too close for her comfort. "How are you doing, Kendall? You seem better than last time I saw you." His voice lowered, "I know losing someone can be rough."

Kendall stepped back, allowing his hand to fall from her arm. *What's going on?* "Yeah, I'm better, better than I was."

He nodded. "We should catch up. Maybe have coffee?"

Is Luke Abbington asking me out? No fucking way. The puking sensation, from last time she was around him, inched up her throat again. "Oh, I don't know, we have a dinner to go to and . . ." she stammered, letting her words trail off.

Janine nudged her sister. "I don't think he means today, Kendall." Janine teased.

Of course not. "Oh, I mean, well . . ." Kendall realized she had started sounding like a babbling idiot, in front of Luke Abbington.

Grandma chimed in. "Kendall, that sounds like fun. You really should get out more. And coffee. I know how much you love coffee. It's a great idea. Kendall, you're probably free tomorrow, right? Because Janine, you've got that thing with your friend, and I'm busy with my brunch club, so Kendall, you're free, right?"

Luke winked at Grandma. "Tomorrow sounds great. Kendall, is Peet's still your favorite?"

Kendall was stunned. How did he remember?

Janine grinned, speaking for her sister. "Oh, she still loves Peet's. Her favorite is the one downtown, right Kendall?"

Her new independent adult sister was starting to get a bit ahead of herself. "Yeah," was the only word Kendall managed to say, moving her hand absentmindedly through her hair.

Luke said, "Tomorrow, 9 a.m. at Peet's, downtown?"

Kendall felt the heat of the Earth's core as the three focused their eyes on her. She shrugged. "Sure, why not." Kendall forced the best smile she could, despite her rattling nerves. Why was she so nervous? She hadn't had feelings for him since . . . since she'd met George.

Luke flashed a smile, revealing his perfect, white teeth. They were bright against his olive skin and dark five o'clock shadow. "I look forward to it. Well, then I'll see you tomorrow. Grandma and Janine," he dipped his head at them, "it was great to finally meet you."

Kendall mumbled, "Bye."

Grandma and Janine hollered, "You too," and waved as they strolled past him.

With Luke out of sight and out of earshot, Janine declared, "Hubba hubba!"

Grandma said, "I second that. My goodness, he's a handsome one."

Kendall stared at her family in disbelief. What dimension had she entered? George had only been gone for six months, and her family was pimping her out to Luke Abbington, of all people. Like she had the energy to spend on the disaster that would be her and Luke Abbington. Irwin Dratch's trial started in less than a month, and it was bringing back a rush of emotions that she'd thought she'd buried.

But then again, maybe she was making too much of this. Maybe Luke wanted to discuss that grief counseling group. Or maybe it was about a job opportunity, since they were both in the same line of work. Maybe he didn't even really want to have coffee, and he was simply being nice and hadn't thought she'd actually take him up on his offer. Then again, she hadn't taken him up on the offer; her sister and grandma had. Why had she agreed?

Kendall joined in on their sudden revelation of Luke's charming presence. "He's all right, I guess."

Janine cracked up. "Oh, my Goddess. You know denial's not just a river in Egypt, right?" And Janine continued to laugh. "Not to mention, I saw the way you looked at him. He makes you flustered, big time. I saw you doing that thing you do with your hair and trying to avoid eye contact with him. You know he's gorgeous, so what's the big deal? Why are you fighting it?"

Had she been *that* transparent? "It's just, I don't know. It's just ..."

Grandma replied, "Just what, dear?"

"Too soon, don't you think?" Part of her thought that it would always be too soon for Luke Abbington.

Grandma said, "It's just coffee, and he seems like a very sweet man. I think it's not too soon. But if it's too soon for you, then don't go. Nobody's rushing you. But it wouldn't hurt to get back out there, and again, it's only coffee, my sweet. You never know, maybe he'll make you laugh."

She couldn't imagine Luke making her laugh at this point in her life. The only laughter Luke conjured was of the memory of how foolish she'd been when she was young and he'd charmed her into his bed.

Janine piped in. "I don't want to force you, but if you don't want to go, I know where I'll be at nine o'clock tomorrow. I wouldn't mind a bite of that yummy man candy. So, what's it gonna be?"

Kendall exhaled. "Fine. I'll go. Now, enough about that. Let's go to the restaurant. It's time to celebrate your graduation, Miss Computer-Scientist-Graduate-of-UC-Berkeley." *Celebrate, yes. Talk about Luke Abbington? No, thank you.*

CHAPTER THIRTEEN

KENDALL

KENDALL INHALED THE SCENT OF FRESHLY GROUND COFFEE before surveying the interior of the coffee shop. Nearly all of the tables were taken, but not by Luke. She stepped aside and stood next to a display filled with a variety of coffee, tea, and mugs for sale. Kendall had arrived early. She figured if she hadn't left the house when she did, she would've talked herself right out of meeting with Luke. It was all just too weird.

A trio of fingers touched her lower back. She swallowed and turned and looked up at Luke. He smiled and said, "Hi."

She mumbled, "Hi." *What is happening? Are those butter-flies? How did they get in there?*

Luke extended his arm. "Shall we?"

She nodded and approached the line toward the register to order coffee. She stood in front of the cashier all too aware of how close Luke was standing beside her. She could feel the heat rise in her cheeks.

The barista in her coffee-bean-colored apron said, "Good morning. Welcome to Peet's. What can I get you?"

Kendall said, "I'll have a caramel latte, please."

Luke stepped forward and placed a hand on her lower back. "And I'll have a cappuccino."

Kendall felt electricity shooting through her body. How on earth did he still have this effect on her?

After the barista rang up their beverages, Luke led her to a small, round table designed for two. She sat across from him, staring into the distance, unable to bring herself to focus on the man that had, somehow, walked right back into her life.

Was she making too much of this? She could feel him watching her, as she stared out the window. Not liking the silence, she finally looked at him and said, "So, did you have a busy morning?"

He shrugged a shoulder, not averting his attention, not trying to look away, not focusing on anyone else but her. "It wasn't too busy. Went to the gym and then headed over here. How about you?"

His answer was short and sweet, but it was supposed to have been longer, filling up the silence that was now present once again. "Oh, not too busy for me either."

He smiled, not speaking, and pressed his lips together, raising his eyebrows, as if wanting her to talk more, as if wanting to listen to . . . her.

She continued speaking, "I was just going over some papers that my realtor gave me." She licked her lips. "I'm thinking of selling the house."

The barista called out, "Luke and Kendall." Kendall flinched, startled by hearing their names spoken together.

Luke said, "I'll get them." Poised and calm, he left the table, giving Kendall a brief moment to collect herself.

She watched his six-foot-three frame move gracefully toward the coffee bar. Fire began to burn in her belly, but she quickly put it out. How was it that he could still elicit any effect on her? Their relationship had been so long ago. Yet here he was, and she felt like it was 2009 all over again. She averted her gaze before he could notice her studying him.

He sat the latte in front of her and, with a boyish grin, said, "Here you go."

"Thank you."

"You were saying that you're planning to sell your house?"

She took a sip of her latte, letting the caramel warmness flow down her throat. "Yeah, the house is kind of big for me, and it's too much of a reminder." She placed her cup down gently, cupping it with her hands. "I probably sound crazy. It's in a great neighborhood, but every time I drive past the spot where he was killed, I . . . I just can't be in that neighborhood anymore." She took another sip, unable to look at Luke.

He said. "I know it's hard. I'm sorry you're going through this. If it makes you feel any better, I also moved out of my house after my wife passed. It was too much of a reminder of a life I didn't have anymore. I ended up renting it out and buying an apartment in San Francisco." She looked up at him, meeting his words with her gaze as he spoke. "I have such a different life now than I thought I would have at my age."

Hearing him speak of losing his wife somehow made her feel understood. Maybe she should've attended grief groups; it was comforting to talk to someone who knew what she was going through. Never in a million years would she have thought the person comforting her would be Luke Abbington—the man who ripped her heart out and stuffed it in a garbage disposal and flipped the switch. Not that he knew how she'd felt back then. She hadn't had the nerve, at the time, to tell him about how she'd been heartbroken when he'd ended things with her.

"I've looked at some places in San Francisco to be closer to work. It would be nice to not have a commute."

"What neighborhoods are you touring?"

"Mainly the Financial District. Might as well be right by work, I'm not terribly interested in utilizing city buses or Muni."

"All work and no play. That's no fun."

"Fun hasn't been my priority lately," she admitted. Maybe Grandma was right. She should be getting out more.

Over the last six months, she barely did more than hang around the house or go to work. Mostly she'd thrown herself into her job. It at least kept her mind off of the huge part of her life that was now missing and gone forever. Occasionally she would go to dinner with a friend, upon their insistence that she leave the house. Really, the only people she spoke to regularly were Janine, Grandma, and Detective Rogers. She supposed it wasn't entirely healthy to spend so much of her time with the detective charged with working her husband's case.

Was it keeping her from moving on? Every time she heard the latest update from the detective, she was transported to that day in the hospital when she saw George lying on the table, lifeless.

Luke set his coffee down. "Maybe we should change that, Kendall. What do you like to do for fun? Do you still like to travel and hike?"

He remembered? "Well, I do like to travel, although I haven't traveled in quite some time, and I do like to hike, to be outside in nature, but I haven't gotten out much lately. I mostly stay home and read. How about you? What have you been up to for the last, oh, ten-ish years?"

Luke scratched his forehead. "I've been working a lot. When Grace was diagnosed with non-Hodgkin's lymphoma, that pretty much consumed our lives. Before that, we did quite a bit of traveling. In fact, a month before she was diagnosed, we went down to South America and the Galapagos Islands." Luke leaned back, grabbed his cup with both hands, and stared at his drink, as if remembering the trip. "I would love to go back one day."

Kendall wondered something, and without holding back, she asked, "I assume you don't have any kids, right?" He hadn't mentioned any while talking about traveling, but as soon as the words left her lips, she regretted them, hoping she hadn't overstepped. "Pets?"

His lips turned into a casual smile, easing Kendall's sudden embarrassment. "No, no kids."

Relief sank into her stomach. Was she hoping he didn't have any kids? Not that Luke wouldn't have the most gorgeous babies. She couldn't believe she was thinking about babies and Luke in the same sentence. She was beginning to believe her barista had added a splash of madness to her latte.

With a one-shoulder shrug, Luke continued, "Grace and I had been trying to conceive for a little while prior to her diagnosis. It was actually why she went to the doctor. We weren't having any luck in the fertility department, and that's when they discovered the cancer."

He bent forward, slumping, and scratched his nose. Kendall couldn't see directly into his eyes, but the way his face fell, the sadness was unmistakable. Kendall resisted the urge to reach out to him.

Luke glanced across the table with what looked like his best attempt at a smile. "Looks like you need a refill on your coffee. Can I get you another?"

"That would be great." She wanted to turn around and watch him walk away as he headed back to the barista, but she didn't. It felt wrong, being with another man somewhere, without George. It was decidedly a date and it was strange. Why wasn't she running away? Maybe she had been lonelier than she'd thought. She did miss the companionship of a warm and loving man. She missed George.

She wasn't sure she was ready to admit it to herself, but she was enjoying her time with Luke. His charisma and witty conversation had always sucked her in.

When she was young, she'd been defenseless against his charm. She was twenty-five and foolish enough to think that she may have a future with Luke. He was older and gorgeous. Intelligent, funny, and thoughtful. The whole package, except for one tiny detail. He was married. She'd kept her crush secret, knowing he wasn't an option. But then his marriage hit a bump and he moved out of the home Grace and he shared. He filed for legal separation. She convinced herself that fate had twisted things and he'd married the wrong woman. In her mind, Luke would get divorced, and Luke and Kendall would live happily ever after. *Silly girl.* About a month into their intense relationship, Luke had ended things rather abruptly. He and Grace were going to give their marriage another shot. When Luke had told her, she'd felt like the air had been knocked out of her. She acted like it wasn't a big deal, when in reality she'd been devastated.

She thought she'd never get over Luke, but she had. *Mostly.* There was still a tiny piece of those feelings somewhere deep down inside of her, and she realized that now. But when she was with George, he made her nearly forget Luke. *Nearly.*

Luke returned with her coffee and sat down. "Maybe we can think of a more cheerful topic." His brown eyes sparkled. "How are things at Bay Star Investments? You've been there since you left our old company, right? Hopefully, it's not filled with weirdos like at our old company?"

She chuckled. "No, no weirdos, thankfully."

"Do you remember that guy that used to take everyone's garbage cans? It was so bizarre. Wait, weren't you friends with him?" he teased.

She failed to suppress a smile. "No, we were not friends,

thank you very much. Actually, I heard he's still at that company; apparently, he had a condition and that's why he was stealing everybody's garbage cans. How crazy is that?"

Luke's head fell back as he laughed. She'd forgotten how easy it was to talk to him. Seeing him laugh made her remember all the mornings she couldn't wait to get to work just to be around him. His laughter was contagious.

"Oh well, we're all a little different, aren't we?"

Kendall fidgeted in her seat. "I suppose."

"Actually, I'm quite hungry. I didn't eat before meeting you here." Luke licked his lips. "There's a great brunch place around the corner. Would you like to join me?"

"Just coffee" was about to turn into more of a date than it already was. What should she do? What she *should* do and what she *ought* to do were two different things.

She opened her mouth to reply, but her phone buzzed in her purse. "Hold that thought," she said, buying time for her decision. There were very few people who called her these days, so it was probably important, or it was just her sister being nosey.

She pulled her phone out of her tote. Observing the caller ID, Kendall swallowed. It was Detective Rogers.

She slid out of her seat, excusing herself, and went over to the shelf of coffees and teas.

"Hi, Detective."

"Hi, Kendall, are you at home?"

She gazed back at Luke, who was watching her from his seat. "No, I'm at coffee with . . . a friend." Why had she said *friend?*

"We have some new evidence on the case. If you can, I'd really appreciate it if you could meet me down here at the station."

Kendall was surprised. "New evidence? What kind of evidence?"

"I can't talk about it on the phone. It's best for you to come down to the station. We have a few questions for you."

Questions, for me? "I can be down there in twenty minutes. I just need to finish up here."

"Thank you, Kendall. We'll see you soon."

She hung up the phone, and her heart pounded.

New evidence? Questions for her? What could they possibly ask her? George's death was a hit-and-run. The driver had been indicted. The police had the evidence.

She headed back to the table and stopped when she reached Luke's chair.

Luke gazed up at her. "Everything all right?"

Allowing the fluster of feelings to roll through her, she finally said, "I'm so sorry, I have to leave." She slowly walked over to her chair and grabbed her tote, still trying to figure out what new evidence the detective could've discovered.

"Raincheck on brunch?"

"Oh right," Kendall said, coming back to reality. "Yes. That would be nice."

There it was. She was being asked on a second date by Luke Abbington while rushing off to the police station to hear of new evidence in her husband's death investigation. At this point, it couldn't get any stranger, right?

Before she left, Luke embraced her in a friendly hug. His warm body and the scent of his spicy aftershave confused Kendall even more.

He released her, and she waved, exiting the coffee shop.

Would her life ever be normal again?

CHAPTER FOURTEEN

MARCUS

Marcus sighed as he placed his cell phone face down onto his desk. "She's on her way now."

Gates tipped his chin. "Good. We need to get this over with. We have a full caseload over here. The sooner we close the George Davis case, the better off we'll be."

Marcus wasn't as convinced as his partner that they'd be able to close the case in the near future. He had a feeling it was just the beginning. With the new evidence, it was clear to him that the accident was no accident. And he would prove it beyond a reasonable doubt.

But what he couldn't figure out was why Irwin Dratch wanted to kill George Davis. They hadn't come up with any specific motives as of yet. Of course, usually, people killed for one of two things: love or money. If Marcus had to guess, he'd say it had to do with money. But they wouldn't know for sure until they started the background check on George Davis. He hated that he had to bring Kendall down to the station to rehash everything. She'd worked hard to put the tragedy behind her.

But when someone is killed, you must interview the spouse. Every armchair detective knew that, as did he. He also had a nagging feeling that this was Day Zero of the investigation of a homicide that happened more than six months ago. He'd been fairly thorough at instructing the crime scene technicians to collect every scrap of evidence, but six months was a long time ago. What had they missed?

Something had felt off about this particular case from the beginning, but he'd ignored it when they arrested Irwin Dratch. What had Dratch been doing that morning? They'd never gotten him to confess why he was out in Davis's neighborhood that day. The powers that be didn't seem to care either. They had the perp for the hit-and-run and that was all that mattered. Now that they knew George Davis's murder was intentional, it made sense why Irwin Dratch had stolen the Lincoln Town Car.

The pieces were beginning to fall into place. Dratch had stolen the car to kill George Davis, dropped off the car in a neighborhood thirty minutes away, and had a vehicle waiting for him. This was premeditated, no question. But now it could take weeks to sift through George's life in an attempt to connect him to Irwin Dratch.

Marcus stood up when he saw Kendall walk toward him. He extended his hand. "Hello, Kendall, thanks for coming down as quickly as you did."

"Not a problem."

Marcus nodded toward the hallway. "I'll be the one to interview you today, let's head into the room down the hall. Please follow me."

Kendall agreed and followed him into interrogation room one, a small room with a table and two chairs. It was chilly, and Marcus could tell by the way Kendall rubbed her arms, that she felt the air conditioning that was pumping through the air vents. Marcus forced a reassuring smile. "Please, sit down. I'm sorry to have to interrupt your day, but I thought you should hear the latest evidence. Due to this new evidence, we have some questions for you that we hope will help us with the investigation."

Kendall shook her head, clearly not understanding. "What is this new evidence? I thought you had Irwin Dratch for George's death?"

"Yes, we do. Irwin Dratch is definitely our number one suspect. But as we were preparing for trial, we reviewed witness statements and the district attorney asked us to talk to your neighbors, once again, to confirm they'd be willing to testify under oath that they saw the Lincoln that morning. While talking with them, we realized some of your neighbors, the Berrys, had not been home during the first round of canvassing. When we asked Mrs. Berry if they remembered anything out of the ordinary that morning, Mrs. Berry remembered an old Town Car had been parked in front of their house. We believe, based on the description, it was the same car that hit George."

"I don't understand. Why was Dratch parked in front of their house before hitting George? Why would he do that?"

"We think Dratch was waiting for him."

Kendall stiffened. "Why would he do that?"

Marcus continued calmly. "That's what we intend to find out. Currently, we think the hit-and-run was intentional and premeditated. In addition to the new witness statement about the parked car, four houses down from the scene of the accident, the DNA evidence came back on some of the other evidence collected. We had analyzed cigarette butts found along the street, including in front of your neighbor's house, where the car was parked, as well as cigarette butts collected where the Lincoln Town Car was dumped, and they were a match. All of this separately may not seem like a lot of evidence. However, when we put it together, we have someone who stole a vehicle, waited near the scene of the accident, dumped the murder weapon—the car—and had a getaway car waiting for him. This all points to premeditated murder."

Marcus watched Kendall's reaction. She shook her head in what seemed like disbelief. Surprise. Confusion.

He believed she didn't know her husband had been murdered. Her reaction was too authentic.

"Why would this man do this to George?"

"That's the part we're having a difficult time with. Unfortunately, this evidence just came in, and we haven't been able to connect George and Dratch, but we haven't received all of George's background check yet. We didn't realize this was a murder investigation six months ago. Now we do. It's almost as if we're starting over. We now have to support a capital murder charge, but without a motive, it will be difficult to prove. The trial will certainly be delayed, but we're trying to act quickly to resolve this in a timely manner. Since we're looking at capital murder, we need to make sure our evidence is air tight."

Kendall sat silently.

Marcus turned over the mugshot of Irwin Dratch. He slid it across the table to Kendall. "Are you sure you've never met him before? Maybe you've seen him around town? Maybe at a park or at the grocery store?"

Kendall delicately picked up the 8x10 photo and studied it.

Marcus didn't sense recognition in her facial expression. It looked more like anger mixed with frustration.

She set the photo down. "No."

Marcus flipped the photo back over. Now for the hard part. He sucked in a breath and exhaled. "Kendall, is there any reason anyone would want to hurt George?"

Kendall seemed to be searching her mind for anybody who may have wanted to harm her husband. She shook her head. "No. I can't. I can't think of anyone."

"How about his work? He worked in finance, right? Maybe a deal had gone bad, or he had an unhappy investor . . ."

She furrowed her brow. "No, he wasn't in that type of finance. He was a comptroller, overseeing the accounting department."

Marcus jotted down notes on his yellow pad of paper. "What about neighbors. Were there any problems with the neighbors? Maybe there was some kind of dispute."

"No. Our neighbors are great." Kendall shook her head and leaned back in a defeated manner. "I don't remember ever hearing an unkind word from any of them, to me or to George. Pretty typical all-American neighborhood. There were barbecues and block parties. All the neighbors got along."

Marcus took additional notes, then he spoke softly, "Now I have to ask some more sensitive questions. I apologize, but I have to do this."

She didn't blink. "That's fine."

Marcus took a breath. *Here goes.* "Did your husband have any recent altercations, such as at a bar?"

Kendall crossed her arms, and squeezed as if trying to keep warm. "Not that I'm aware of. He didn't really go out to bars very much. At least not with me. Maybe after work with some other folks from the company? I don't really know. He certainly never came home with bruises or cuts or anything that would indicate he'd been in a fight. He wasn't a big drinker either. He is—was—kind of a health nut."

Marcus watched as a flicker of fond remembrance danced across Kendall's face, and then it disappeared.

"Health nut. How so? Did he go to the gym a lot? Maybe somebody had it in for him at the gym . . ."

"Well, he ran every morning, obviously. He went to the gym three days a week. He had a green smoothie every single day. No trans fats in our house. He also didn't like that I had a bit of a sweet tooth. I'd bring home cookies and ice cream, and he would give me a hard time. He'd say I was going to get diabetes and every other disease because of all the sugar." Kendall slumped back into her chair.

"Okay. How about any vices? Gambling?"

Kendall shook her head no.

"What about money problems? How are things financially for you and your husband? Were you having any issues paying your mortgage or the car payments or anything like that?"

Kendall stiffened a bit. "We didn't have money problems. Quite the opposite actually. He made good money, as do I. We were more than comfortable."

Marcus wondered why it made her uncomfortable to discuss her financial situation. He took note to look extra hard at their financials.

"Had George ever been unfaithful to you?"

"Not that I'm aware of. I mean, George and I were good, solid. I'm fairly confident he wasn't having an affair and hadn't ever cheated on me."

"George sounds like he was an amazing guy."

Kendall stared off at the wall behind Marcus. "He was."

"Were *you* always faithful to George?"

Her voice shook. "Yes, I was always faithful to George. Once we got together, there was nobody else. He treated me like a queen, supported my career, and embraced my faults, other than the sugar addiction. I would've never been unfaithful to him."

Marcus watched her expression carefully and tapped the end of his pen on his notepad. If there were no affairs, no gambling, no money problems, no beef with the neighbors or strangers, and no known issues at work, what could it be? Something wasn't adding up.

"Was George acting any differently leading up to the days or the weeks before the accident?"

She pinched her lips together. "No."

Kendall sat silently.

After a few minutes of Marcus and Kendall sitting in the quiet room, she began to speak, "Things were great. We were planning a trip for our five-year wedding anniversary." She stopped and took a few breaths. "He was so excited. Both of us had small families. If it was solely up to him, he'd have had a whole house full of kids." She chuckled slightly and rubbed her arms more.

Marcus knew he needed to tread lightly. He wasn't sure how much more Kendall could take. The personal questions and forcing her to think back to a life that no longer existed for her, felt cruel.

Having kept in touch with Kendall, he had noticed a positive change in her demeanor after she resumed work. Would this line of questioning throw her into a backward spiral?

This had to be one of the most difficult interviews he'd done in his career. Making people relive the worst time of their lives was not for the faint of heart. He cleared his throat. "Were there any changes to his routine at all? Sleeping habits? Exercise? Work?"

She answered quietly. "No. No changes."

"How about with his family? He has a brother, are they close?"

"No, not really. His brother lives down south, in Bakersfield, with his mother. George called his mom every week to see how she was doing. She hasn't been in good health for quite some time. But George and his brother have never been close, not even in childhood. His mother described them as oil and water."

"Had he spoken to his brother or mother more recently?"

"Nothing more than his weekly phone call to his mother."

"Any change to her health or her situation before George's death?"

"No, not really."

"Have you talked to his family since his he's been gone?"

"I call his mother every few weeks to see how she is. I think she's declining rather quickly now . . ." Kendall bowed her head and he saw a tear drop fall.

Marcus scribbled down this new information on his notepad. "Is there anything else you can think of that could have tied George to Irwin Dratch or any reason why anybody would want to harm him?"

She answered hopelessly, "No."

Marcus closed his notepad. "Those are all the questions I have for today. I'm sorry for interrupting your coffee. You said you were out with your sister? Or a friend?"

Kendall's expression changed. She seemed to have clammed up. What was that about?

She said, "I was with an old friend. It's no problem. Anything I can do to help."

For the first time, Marcus sensed that Kendall wasn't telling him everything. What was she hiding?

"Great. We appreciate your cooperation and help with the case. How are Janine and your Grandma doing?" It felt odd to ask her these casual questions after putting her through the wringer.

Kendall seemed to relax. "Janine's great. Her commencement ceremony was yesterday. She already has a job lined up at a startup in Berkeley. She's pretty excited. Grandma loves the new retirement community. Lots of brunch and book club. The dementia has gotten a little worse, but thankfully, she has mostly good days."

"Great, please tell them I said hello, and I hope everything keeps going well." Marcus paused before adding, "Let me know if you can think of anything, anything at all that'll help. Don't hesitate to call me, no matter the time."

He led her out of the interrogation room and back out to the main office area. As he watched her exit the building, he wondered why it had struck a nerve with her when he'd asked about her coffee companion. It was as if she was hiding something. But what?

CHAPTER FIFTEEN

LUKE

Before knocking on Kendall's front door, Luke smoothed down the sides of his royal blue blazer. He clutched a small bouquet of white calla lilies in his right hand; he was ready. The door swung open, and he was struck by the gorgeous figure. Kendall's black wraparound dress, with a low neckline, hit right above the knee. Her face lit up. "Hi," she said, with anxious-like laughter.

His pulse raced. "You look stunning."

"Oh, thank you. You look amazing too."

He presented her with the flowers. "These are for you."

She stepped back and stared at them. "This is so thoughtful." Kendall turned around and motioned for him to come in. "I'll put these in a vase before we go, so they don't dry out."

He stepped over the threshold and glanced around her living room. There were moving boxes piled up against the walls, and her sister was lounging on the sofa. Kendall looked over her shoulder. "You remember Janine, right?"

"Yes, of course. Hi, Janine, it's good to see you."

Janine grinned. "You too." She glanced over at Kendall and

sat up. "Wait, did you bring her flowers? Did you bring candy, too?"

Luke watched as Janine winked at Kendall. Was that a good sign? He thought so. "No, no candy, just flowers. Did I totally blow it?"

Janine shifted on the sofa. "I don't know. I think maybe. Only time will tell." She shrugged and chuckled playfully.

"Then wish me luck." He swallowed a nervous lump in his throat and followed Kendall into her kitchen. He admired her backside as she reached above for a vase from a top cabinet. God, he'd love for them to spend a romantic night at his place, but obviously, it was too soon for that.

They'd only had one coffee date and talked on the phone a few times and texted daily over the last week, but it was still too soon for anything more. He was more than ready to take their newfound relationship, or whatever this was, to the next level, but he wasn't convinced she was as ready as he was.

Unable to resist fully, he approached Kendall at the sink as she filled the vase with water. He placed his hand on her lower back and whispered, "Anything I can do to help?"

She didn't flinch from his touch, and he could hear her catch her breath. *Definitely a good sign*, he thought. She turned to face him. "No, thanks. I've got it." She set the flowers on the counter and faced him with her full body. He could see the cleavage down her dress. Oh, the things he wanted to do to her.

"Would you like a drink before we head out? I have wine and probably some whiskey and maybe gin?" she asked.

"That's a tempting offer, but I don't want to miss our reservation."

She nodded and grabbed her purse from the table.

He extended his hand and said, "Shall we?"

He watched her contemplate whether or not to put her hand in his. Maybe he shouldn't have assumed she'd feel comfortable by his gesture. But if he removed his offer, it would make for an awkward start to the date. His mouth went dry as a second passed, a second that felt like minutes. Relief sank in once she placed her hand in his. It fit like a glove.

On the way out of the house, they waved to Janine. "You two crazy kids have fun!" she called out.

He handed his key to the valet, stepped out of his new BMW, and met Kendall on the sidewalk outside of the Jani Franko restaurant in San Francisco. He was pulling out all the stops for her. She was deserving of more than three Michelin stars, if they existed.

"Have you been here before?" he asked her, this time offering her his elbow to escort her, rather than his hand, and walking in.

"No, but I've heard it's great. You?"

He gazed into her emerald green eyes. "No, not yet. I'd been waiting for a special occasion."

The host squeezed them into a table for two. He wished he could see her better; the restaurant bordered on too dark. He couldn't believe they were finally out on a real date. She was as beautiful as he remembered from all those years ago. Smart. Sexy. Gorgeous. She was the whole package.

She grimaced at him. "What's the matter?"

"It's so dark in here. I can barely see you. How will I know if you pop out and have another person take your place?"

She laughed and his heart smiled. "I guess you won't."

He wished he'd picked a better-lit restaurant, but she seemed to be having a good time, so he figured it was probably fine.

A waiter approached in a dark suit and a starched white

shirt. He reminded Luke of a character from the Munsters. It was as if no smiles were allowed. The waiter asked which menu they'd be choosing for the evening: the three-, four-, or five-course, and with or without wine pairing.

He looked across at Kendall. "What do you think? Should we go for the whole thing? The five-course with wine pairing—that is, if you're up for it?"

Kendall seemed apprehensive. "I don't know. It seems like a lot. What do you think?" She glanced up at the waiter, who seemed to roll his eyes as he explained that the portions were modest and elegant in size.

Her eyes, which twinkled over the candlelight, darted to Luke. "Okay . . . I'm up for the challenge."

The waiter nodded and left to retreat to what Luke could only assume was a dungeon, based on his demeanor and grim attitude. Shortly after, another member of the vampire family returned with complimentary flutes of champagne.

Luke raised his glass. "To old friends?"

She paused briefly before she nodded. "To old friends."

What was that? She seemed to not like the term old friends. Sure, they'd been more than friends for a short period of time. Had he hurt her more than she had let on all those years ago? He watched her sip the bubbly and set the glass back down. "I didn't realize Janine was staying with you. How's that going?"

Kendall relaxed her posture. "She moved in after . . . the accident. Not accident." She shook her head as if to make the thoughts fall away. "Sorry. Yes, she's staying with me until the move. And then I'll move into my new place, and she'll move into her own place for the first time. She's excited to be out on her own, which I can understand. I vaguely remember being twenty-two, fresh out of college, and free to do as I pleased." She gazed ahead as if remembering fondly.

He remembered her being fresh out of college as well. That

was when they met. For her, it was her first job out of college, and he took notice of her immediately. There was something special about Kendall Murphy. He knew it then—and he knew it now.

THEIR CONVERSATION WAS EASY AND FUN. WHEN THE fifth course and fifth wine pairing arrived, she teased, "I'm not sure about all this wine. I'm beginning to think you're trying to get me drunk."

He feigned surprise. "I hadn't realized that was an option?"

She laughed, and he chided himself for wishing he could skip the dancing and take her back to his place.

They strolled out of the restaurant hand in hand. As they walked down the sidewalk, he felt the buzz of his cell phone in his blazer pocket, but ignored it, not wanting to appear rude.

They stopped, and he turned to face her. "Are you ready for the surprise?"

She gritted her teeth, playfully peered up at him sideways. "Yes, I think?"

The buzzing in his coat returned. Who on earth was calling? Dread filled his belly. *Goddammit. It better not be him.*

She noticed the buzzing. "Do you need to take that?"

"No, it's fine."

"Don't be silly, just take the call. It's totally fine. Trust me." She gave him a reassuring nod.

He stepped away and pulled out his phone. As he feared, it was him. He spoke in a hushed tone. "What do you want?"

"You know what I want. And I'm not going to stop until I get it."

"If you don't stop calling me, you'll regret it." Anger seared through Luke.

"I'm afraid you're the one who will regret it if I don't get my money."

Luke demanded. "For the last time. Leave me alone."

He hung up the call and turned off the phone. He took a few breaths before returning to Kendall. He didn't want her to see him rattled. He needed to put that unpleasantness out of his mind.

He grinned at Kendall. "Okay, where were we? Oh yes, the surprise that you're not quite sure you're ready for." He put his hand on her right hip and extended his left in the air.

A grin spread across her face. She placed her left hand on his chest and placed her right in his left. He wasn't sure if he could form words. Being this close to her was a true test of his willpower. He whispered, "So, do you know how to dance?"

She stared into his eyes. "I do, a little. Is that the surprise? Are we going dancing?"

"Do you salsa?" He began the movements of a simple step and reached for her hand, and she tilted her head back in laughter, as he twirled her around on the sidewalk.

When he stopped, he said, "We could go to the club or stay here?"

She peered out at the sidewalk and busy street. "Maybe we should head to the club."

"As you wish."

Luke would focus on Kendall and her needs. He would go at her pace. She was what he wanted, and there was no way he would let anything or anyone get in the way of their relationship. He let her go once. It was a mistake he would not repeat.

After an evening of salsa, Luke insisted on walking Kendall to the front door. She stopped when they approached the porch and swiveled around to face him. He was surprised and proud of himself that he'd managed to not seem too eager as they danced the very seductive dance of salsa all night, but now, standing in the moonlight, he couldn't resist a moment more.

He took a step toward her, placed his hands on her hips, and gently pulled her close. He shut his eyes and pressed his lips to hers. She wrapped her arms around his neck, and he squeezed her tighter. The kiss started gentle, but soon it turned more passionate. He began to probe her mouth with his tongue and his body was overcome with desire for her. He forced himself to behave. He didn't want their relationship to be based solely on sexual desire. He had to wait. That was the plan, but as she grew breathless, he wondered what would happen if he threw his plan straight out the window. She was far too important to him to take any chances.

He moved his hands from her waist to her face and cupped her cheeks. "I had a wonderful time tonight." He kissed her softly once more. It took every ounce of resolve for him to step back. "I'll call you, okay?"

She nodded with a shy grin.

"Good night, Kendall."

"Good night."

He strolled back to his car with a beaming smile across his face. In his gut, he knew she was his and he was hers.

CHAPTER SIXTEEN

KENDALL

KENDALL SLAPPED HER LEG, DOUBLING OVER IN LAUGHTER. Beth continued to tell a story about one of her latest dating failures. "And imagine my surprise when I strutted through his front door, ready for some action, only to find out that not only did he have six cats, which by the way did not seem friendly at all, I mean these were like a gang of junkyard cats, but the apartment is decorated floor to ceiling with cats: cat paintings, cat figurines, photos of cats. Cats! And, woman, that's why I no longer date a guy who says he likes cats." Beth pursed her lips and arched her brow before draining the glass of white wine in her hand.

Kendall dabbed the corners of her eyes with the back of her hand. Once composed, she took a sip of her Riesling. "That's hilarious. Note to self: don't date guys who hang with junkyard cats!" Sitting on the sofa with her closest friend, drinking wine and talking about dating, felt normal. It was nice to feel normal again. It helped that she had started sleeping through the night and exercising at the gym again. The darkness that had taken over her life was beginning to lift. She could see that reassuring ray of sunshine poking through the gloomy clouds.

Beth tucked a strand of bright-blue hair behind her ear and squinted at Kendall. "Exactly." She refilled her glass with the bottle sitting on the coffee table and said, "You know, Kendall, it's nice to see you smile again. I'm sorry I haven't been around more. I've been busy with my latest project, and it seemed like you needed some time."

Kendall shook her head. "Oh, stop. There's no reason for an apology. I know you tried to be around. I wasn't up for normal fun, I guess. I'm glad you came over today and decided to drink with me."

"Woman, if you ever need someone to drink with, you know I'll be here." Beth winked.

Yes, she could always count on Beth to have a good time. A lot of people misinterpreted Beth. They saw the tattoos and blue hair and thought she wasn't serious or intelligent, but they were wrong. Beth was a talented and successful graphic artist, who was also one of the most fearless, loyal, kind, and outspoken people she had ever known. The day she met Beth in the dorms freshman year, Kendall's life changed, even though she didn't know it at the time. To the outside world, the two of them looked like opposites. Beth was the single artist living in the city, and Kendall was the financial analyst living in the suburbs with a white picket fence and plans for 2.4 children. Kendall had always admired Beth's tenacity and confidence to be unapologetically who she was at the core. She wished she could be more like Beth. If Beth were rainbow-colored ice cream, Kendall was the vanilla sprinkles. Maybe it was time she started to change that?

Kendall said, "I'm beginning to feel like myself again."

"That's awesome. But it seems like maybe it's something else too. If I didn't know better, I'd think something, or someone, was up."

Kendall wondered if she was *that* obvious. Was her sudden

mood change because of Luke? She knew that he'd reignited a quenched flame inside of her that she thought was long gone. Being with him, it was as if no time had passed. It was as if the feelings she had for Luke had been buried in an imaginary chest that burst open the day he walked back into her life. At times, it was a bit unsettling. Had she latched onto him simply because she was lonely, or were the feelings real?

Kendall's cheeks flushed, from the wine and from thinking about Luke, but she wasn't sure she was ready to share the details about Luke, so she decided to switch subjects. "Well, things have been progressing with the house, and it's almost ready for staging. I plan to put it on the market next week. I've been looking at some places downtown, which I'm kind of excited about. You know, live the life of a city gal, at last. I'm thirty-five and a Bay Area native—and have never lived in the city. We should all do it at least once, right?"

Beth nodded. "Sure. Sure. Sounds exciting. But my spidey sense says maybe there's something else?"

The only people who knew about Luke were her grandmother and her sister. She feared what people would think about her dating so soon after George's passing. She set down her empty glass. "Well, I started seeing someone."

Beth's mouth gaped open. "What? When? Who? All the questions!"

Kendall's heart rate quickened. "His name is, uh, Luke Abbington, formerly known as 'he who shall not be named.' I bumped into him on the street. We had coffee the next day, and we've gone out four times since."

Beth's mouth dropped open.

Kendall continued, "We call and text, and that's pretty much the whole story."

"He who shall not be named? The man who ripped your heart out, like what . . . how many years ago?"

Kendall spoke softly. "Ten years ago." When she'd dated Luke, for that intense month, she'd never told anyone about him, except Beth. For one, they worked together and for two, it was a bit delicate since he was separated from his wife. She'd never told Beth his real name. First, he was 'the guy' before being renamed 'he who shall not be named' after the rather sudden breakup.

Beth shook her head in disbelief. "Is he still married?"

"No, his wife passed a year or so ago."

Beth adjusted her glasses. "Huh. Have you guys talked about what happened all those years ago?"

Kendall didn't really want to. She didn't want Luke to think she'd been pining for him all these years. "No, we've started from scratch, kind of."

"Kind of?"

"Well, we obviously know one another, but we don't talk about the past."

Beth scrunched her face. "Are you happy?"

Kendall nodded.

Beth shrugged. "Well, then I'll give him the benefit of the doubt then . . .you say his real name is Luke Abbington?" She reached over, picked up her smartphone from the coffee table, and started typing things into it, scrolling and squinting at the screen. A few moments later, Beth held up her phone. "Is this him?"

Kendall studied the screen and a smile crept up her face. "Yeah, that's him."

Beth fanned her face with her hand. "Damn, girl. He's hot." She paused. "Wait, he's not into cats, is he?"

Kendall laughed and almost choked on her wine. "No pets."

"Good." Beth returned her focus to stalking Luke online. She looked up. "How old is he? I mean don't get me wrong, the man is fine, but he looks a bit older."

"A little. He's forty-five."

"So things are going well? No devil horns hiding in that gorgeous dark, wavy hair?"

Kendall sank into the couch. "I haven't found any yet. I mean, I'm not sure of the future, but I *like* him." It was true, and it scared the bejesus out of her.

"Oh, honey, that's great. Of course, I have to meet him to make sure he's good enough and not gonna hurt you again. If he does, I'll find him. You can tell him, he's been warned. When will you see him next?"

"Tonight. He offered to pick me up. He wants to cook me dinner. I told him it was silly, but he insisted."

"And he cooks? Maybe he plans on serving up something special, like Luke à la Kendall."

Kendall chuckled at the thought and wondered if that was what dinner at his place meant. They'd basically only kissed, and it definitely surprised her that Luke hadn't tried to get more physical. Kendall wanted to do more, but hadn't. She'd forgotten what it felt like to want to be close to someone. During those moments, it felt as if the entire world melted away, and the only thing she could think of was him, his body and hers. But was she ready for that? Before she could respond to Beth's insinuation, a rather loud knock on the door startled both of them.

"Is that him, already?" Beth asked.

Kendall turned on the screen to her smartphone; it was only 4 p.m. He wasn't supposed to arrive for two more hours. She said, "I don't think so."

Another very loud rapping on the door made the nerves in Kendall's belly rattle. She hurried to the front door and peered through the peephole. It was Detective Rogers. *That's odd. I didn't expected him to come by. He didn't call. Now that I think about it, I haven't heard from him in over a week.*

She opened the door and quickly saw that it wasn't just

Detective Rogers—but also Detective Gates and a team of a dozen uniformed officers. She said, "What's going on?"

Marcus kept his hands by his side. "Kendall Murphy, we have a warrant to search your home." He handed her a typewritten piece of paper listing the details of the search warrant, with a blank expression on his face.

She tried looking at his eyes, but he stared at the center of her forehead, not looking at her. Why?

What was happening? Why had they ambushed her like this? She'd been apprised of every step of the investigation to date. Why would they be searching her home?

Marcus, finally meeting her eyes with his, said, "Ma'am, we're going to enter the home now. Please stand aside."

Ma'am? She stepped back. Beth rushed to her side. "What's going on?"

"They're searching the house. They have a search warrant." She showed the paper to Beth, as if Beth wouldn't believe her.

"Did you know about this?" she asked.

"No," Kendall replied after the last officer entered. She stood against the living room wall, while the police began searching, and watched in horror and disbelief.

Detective Rogers approached them. "Ms. Murphy, I want you to know everything's fine. We're just following protocol. Please let me know if you have any questions. Also, we'll need you to come down to the station for further questioning. We prefer you to come on your own, willingly."

Willingly? She'd been to the station a dozen times. "I don't . . . I don't understand what you mean. Do you need me to come down right now? I was just there a few weeks ago."

"Ma'am, your husband's case has been officially turned into a homicide investigation. You don't have to come into the station today, but we obviously prefer that you would. Please come down as soon as you can. We have some questions for you."

There was that *ma'am* again. "I don't know what else I can add to the investigation. I feel like I've answered all the questions asked of me, and I've been cooperative. I don't understand why you felt the need to surprise me at my home, with a search warrant."

Marcus . . . Detective Rogers . . . What was she supposed to call him now? He stepped closer. "We have reason to believe that Irwin Dratch was hired to kill your husband. We need to have statements from all potential persons of interest."

Kendall felt like she'd been punched in the stomach. Was she a person of interest? Beth placed her hand on Kendall's shoulder, forcing her to face her. "Kendall, you need to get a lawyer, right now."

Kendall shook her head. "I have nothing to hide."

"Woman, if you ever have to be questioned by the police, you absolutely need a lawyer present. Trust me, I listen to a lot of true crime podcasts, and that is one of the non-breakable rules: *always ask for a lawyer*."

"But I'm not under arrest." She turned to look at Detective Rogers. "I'm not under arrest, right?" Kendall couldn't believe any of this was happening. And that someone had hired Irwin Dratch to kill her husband. Irwin Dratch was a hitman. How was this her life now?

"No. You're not under arrest. We just need to ask you some questions."

Beth insisted. "Kendall, it doesn't matter if you're under arrest or not. You're a potential person of interest, and let's face it, they always suspect the spouse. You need a lawyer with you, even for questioning. Haven't you watched any of the documentaries on Netflix? There's like a new one every week. There are tons of wrongful convictions, usually because the suspect didn't have a lawyer, or didn't have a good lawyer. You never want to be questioned without a lawyer by your side." At that moment,

Beth squared her shoulders to Kendall's, facing away from Detective Rogers, and she lowered her voice. "I know some people. We'll get you hooked up with a freaking awesome attorney. Don't say another word to the officers and don't go down to the station for an interview without the attorney."

Kendall had never seen Beth so serious. She supposed it couldn't hurt to retain counsel. How had she gone from having a normal day of girl time with Beth and anticipating an evening with Luke, to becoming a person of interest in the murder-for-hire plot to kill her husband?

CHAPTER SEVENTEEN

MARCUS

"What time is she coming with her lawyer?" Gates asked.

Marcus didn't glance up from the financial records he was reviewing. "In about an hour." Marcus turned the paper. He didn't believe that Kendall was capable of killing her husband for money. Or was he so blinded by her that he'd made a bad judgment call? He was supposed to be objective, but he hadn't been. He knew everybody was a potential suspect; he just didn't think it applied to her. He thought she was different.

Gates said, "Buddy, don't get so down about the widow. You never know when someone should be winning an Oscar for their performance."

Marcus cocked his head. The look in Kendall's eyes when she stood over her husband lying on the hospital table was too raw, too painful to pretend. Wasn't it? "You saw her man. She was in agony about his death."

"Maybe it was real. Maybe it was regret. Remorse. Maybe it seemed like a good idea to bump off the husband and become an instant multi-millionaire. But then when she saw him, she realized what she'd done and wished to take it back. It happens more than you'd think. But then again, maybe it was real, and she's innocent. But, you know, it's usually the spouse."

Marcus knew the statistics, but something in his gut told him Kendall wasn't capable of the crime. But then again, he hadn't picked up on the fact that the accident was actually a murder-for-hire. Maybe he painted Kendall Murphy all wrong.

"Did you identify the guy who arrived at Kendall's as the search team was leaving the house? He looked awfully cozy with Kendall, potential-motive cozy," Gates said.

Marcus found it strange as well, since Kendall never mentioned she was seeing someone, but she'd been cagey when he'd inquired about her coffee date. Perhaps it was that guy. It'd only been seven months since her husband's death. Was that enough time to find a new love interest?

Or had she loved the guy all along and killed her husband so that she could be with him? Maybe Kendall was a cold, calculating woman who had everyone fooled. He supposed that Gates was right. You never really know anyone, not really. He felt stupid for falling for her act, if it was an act. Even now he felt stupid for still believing she couldn't be responsible.

Marcus glanced up when Ronnie approached with a stack of papers. "Hey. What are you carrying?"

Ronnie pushed his dark frames up. "Here's that list of unsolved murders with DNA matches to your guy. It's a long list. My guess is this guy's been killing for a long time. He may be a low-level hitman or a decorated mafia murderer. Either way, he was good at his craft, until now. He's got no record. I'm surprised he didn't skip town when you arrested him the first time."

Gates said, "Ain't that the truth? Unbelievable. Good thinking Rogers, having crime scene collect all those cigarette butts. I think they wanted to strangle you when you insisted they bag all debris on the road within a quarter-mile of the scene. Buddy, that instinct will get you everywhere. Well done."

So, not all of his instincts were off. *Good to know.* But if Dratch was such a great hitman, why hadn't he run? Those types typically squirreled away money for a rainy day. What was keeping him in town?

Thankfully, he and Gates figured out the truth and were able to re-arrest Dratch and charge him with murder before he could skip town. A double thank you to the judge for not granting bail. They had Dratch in custody, and Marcus wasn't letting him out of his sight until the case went to trial.

It would be helpful if Dratch rolled on whoever hired him, but he was continuing his tight-lipped routine. They needed to motivate him to talk, but what could they use to break him?

MARCUS AND GATES SAT ACROSS FROM KENDALL AND HER new lawyer, Cybil Hernandez. By the confidence Ms. Hernandez oozed and the expensive suit, he figured Kendall had gone out and hired the best lawyer money could buy. *Smart. Guilty?*

To his relief, the questioning was nearly over. Kendall had been consistent with all of her answers. Yet she was obviously in distress, biting her lip and fidgeting in her chair. He knew it was natural for a person, whether they were guilty or not, to be in some discomfort during questioning in a murder investigation. Or was she worried they would figure out she was the one who hired Dratch to kill George?

Gates tapped his pen on his notepad. "We have one more question for you before you head out: who was the gentleman who arrived as we were leaving your house on the day of the search? Was it a relative, a friend?"

Marcus watched as Kendall and her lawyer whispered quietly to themselves. He would've paid good money to hear what they were saying.

Her lawyer replied, "We don't see how this is relevant to the investigation, and we choose not to answer."

Gates and Marcus exchanged glances.

Gates attacked. "Not relevant to the investigation? We both know people kill for one of two reasons: one is for love, and the other is for money. Your client is looking at potential motives related to both. If Ms. Murphy was engaged in a relationship during her marriage, prior to her husband's death, it's motive. She just told us, on record, that she hadn't had an extramarital affair. And now there's some guy in the picture, and you think it's irrelevant? I think that man, who is obviously more than a friend, could be quite relevant. You can either answer now and do this the easy way, or we can do it the hard way."

Marcus was glad that Gates took on the bad cop role. He'd gotten far too close to Kendall and her family over the last seven months. It ate him up to see what they were putting her through. Kendall was clearly upset over the questions about this man, but why? Had she been having an affair? Did that mean she was guilty of murder? Maybe not; however, it would make her a liar. If she lied about one thing, she could lie about another —like not killing her husband.

Ms. Hernandez returned from consulting with her client. "His name is Luke Abbington."

Gates folded his arms across his chest. "Now that wasn't so hard. And what is the nature of the relationship between Ms. Murphy and Luke Abbington?"

Cybil began to speak, but Kendall placed her hand on her shoulder and shook her head. She focused on Marcus. "Luke and I ran into each other a few weeks back. It was the day of my sister's graduation. We met the next day, and we've been seeing each other ever since."

"Ran into?" Gates glared at Kendall.

"Luke and I worked together ten years ago, but I hadn't seen him since I left that company. That is, until I ran into him after Janine's commencement. That's it. That's the whole story."

Marcus watched as she continued fidgeting in her chair. Why didn't he believe that she was telling the whole story? Something was off, but what?

Kendall's lawyer shoved a legal pad into her briefcase and then asked, "Do you have any more questions for my client?"

Gates said, "No. Thank you for coming down today. We really appreciate it."

Marcus couldn't meet Kendall's gaze as she and her lawyer hurried out of the interrogation room.

Back at their desks, Gates asked, "You think she's hiding something about this Luke Abbington character?"

"I don't know. But we need to look into him ASAP."

Gates leaned back in his chair. "Based on the financials, she inherited a lot of money when her husband died. If that wasn't enough, all of a sudden, she's got herself a new boyfriend too."

Marcus's face fell.

Gates sighed. "Sorry, buddy, but she's my number one right now. So far, Kendall has the motive and the means to pay someone."

Marcus listened to the words of his partner. However, it still didn't make sense. They still hadn't proved that she had an affair during her marriage, and although she inherited a small fortune between the life insurance, 401(k), stocks, bonds, the house, and savings, she herself had a successful career and her own money.

She didn't really need the extra, as far as he could see. She wasn't in debt. She didn't seem to have a gambling problem or other reason to need a large sum of money.

But what about Luke Abbington? How did Luke Abbington fit into the picture? Had he run into her by chance, or was his involvement part of a bigger scheme?

CHAPTER EIGHTEEN

KENDALL

Kendall paced around her kitchen with her cell phone held up to her ear, listening to it ring. And ring. She stopped pacing when Luke answered. "Hey, it's me."

"Hi, I was just thinking about you," he said casually.

"I just got back from the interview at the station with my new lawyer, and your name came up." Kendall paused, rethinking how she was going to explain her current predicament. It really *wasn't* a fifth date conversation. "They think that dating you creates a motive for me. The entire interview was weird." Kendall's heart thumped in her ears, as she waited for Luke's response.

How had she become a person of interest? What did that even mean? Her lawyer had tried to calm her by explaining that she wasn't officially a suspect, but she could become one if the police thought they had concrete evidence linking her to the crime.

"I'm sure it'll all be okay," Luke said.

"I hope so. I just thought you should hear it from me, in case they call you. They're likely to investigate you because of your connection to me. They seem concerned about our relationship." The word *relationship* felt odd on her tongue. A relationship they really hadn't discussed—not really. Were she and Luke exclusive? She had no idea if Luke was dating other women. Maybe that was why he hadn't been more physical with her.

"Well, I'm about to head into a meeting. How about I come over tonight, and we can talk more about it?"

Her body relaxed. "Okay."

"Perfect. I should arrive around six."

"See you then."

"Bye."

Kendall set her phone down on the kitchen countertop, and her blood pressure shot back up. She needed a glass of wine. The stress was worse than managing a multimillion-dollar portfolio. Was it too early for a drink? She didn't care. Her nerves were shot, and wine was the answer at the moment. She moseyed over to the rack and pulled a cabernet franc. She uncorked the bottle and held it to her nostrils and inhaled. Peppery, with a fruit finish. *Yum.*

After pouring herself a full glass, she leaned against the counter and sipped, while thinking about the investigation. They wouldn't find anything linking her to a murder-for-hire plot, so she shouldn't be worried, right? Then why was she so stressed? How would the case affect her relationship with Luke? In some ways, they were like brand-new. In other ways, not. Could they survive the pressure of a murder investigation? She knew better than most that life could turn on a dime. One minute you could be picking out tropical vacations, and the next, you're burying your husband.

She glanced up to see Janine stomping through the house as usual. "Hey," Kendall said, a little too loud.

Janine headed toward her, spying the unpacked boxes and papers strewn about. "I forgot what a mess this place is now.

The police should provide packing services after what they did. "

"I know, right? I started repacking, but I got distracted. My goal is to clean up and put it on the market ASAP. I really don't know how much longer I can stay in this house."

The place wasn't only a reminder of a life she no longer had, but now it was a disaster too, a crime scene. It was certainly not a place she wanted to be in.

"I know what you mean." Janine averted her gaze and scratched her cheek. "I don't know how you feel about this, and I hate to spring this on you right now, because I know it's been a crazy few weeks, but I think I found an apartment." She glanced up at Kendall. "The only problem is that it's available immediately, and it's so awesome, I fear if I don't jump on it, I could lose it. You know how difficult it is to find a nice place in Berkeley. I wouldn't even consider it right now, but it's practically my dream apartment."

Another punch to the gut. Kendall took a long sip to steady herself. "That's great, Janine. I'm happy for you." She didn't want to take away Janine's happiness. She'd be fine on her own. She'd survived worse.

"But . . . it's just an apartment. I can totally pass on it. You know, I'll stay here with you until the house sells. The realtor said it could go fast, right? I'll find something else." She flipped her hand at Kendall. "Forget I said anything. I'm here for you, anything you need."

Was her fake enthusiasm that apparent? No, she didn't want Janine to move out, but she'd feel awful if her sister passed on her first real apartment. Her dream apartment. Janine was right, the house would sell in a few weeks and she'd find a new place on her own. That was the plan.

Kendall set down her glass and hugged Janine. "Thank you for worrying about me." She slid back. "But don't be silly, you should absolutely take the apartment." Kendall took a seat at the dining table. "Now, I want to see pictures."

Janine's eyes lit up, and she jumped with giddiness. "Okay, it's so awesome!"

While Janine fished her laptop out of her bag, Kendall contemplated her own living situation. Maybe she should stay at a hotel for a while. The idea of room service and a cleaning staff sounded great. She could stay downtown near work. A fresh environment, clean sheets, and no commute. She began to really like the idea.

Janine sat next to her and pointed at the screen. "Look, views of the Berkeley Marina right out my kitchen window! How freaking amazing is that?"

"My gosh, that is amazing. You absolutely have to take it. Actually, maybe I'll take it," she teased.

"So, you're really okay with this?"

Kendall placed her arm around her sister. "Yes, most definitely. And who knows, maybe I'll stay at a hotel for a while—to treat myself."

"That's right. Treat. Yo. Self."

Kendall grinned at her sister. "Fo' sho'. Do you have plans tonight? You seem to have had many nights out recently. Being young is so nice . . ."

"Oh, stop. You're not old. I was invited by some coworkers to see a new band tonight in Oakland. But I can stay here if you want." Janine stopped, and her mouth dropped open. "Oh my gosh, how did you let me go on about the apartment for the last thirty minutes? Wasn't today the day of your interview at the police station?"

Kendall sighed. "Yeah. It was awful." She went on to explain about the interview and how Luke was coming over so they could talk.

"Well then, I'll definitely get out of your hair. I don't want to get in between any of that." She winked.

"Oh, I don't know what you're talking about." She nudged her sister playfully.

Janine eyed her skeptically. "Sure. Well, I better get ready," she said and skittered off.

Kendall hollered, "Love you." She watched her sister rush down the hall to her bedroom and sighed. Soon, it would be the end of a short era. She'd really enjoyed living with Janine. She had such spunk and fire. She lit up every room with her presence. Kendall would miss seeing her sparkly self every day.

The sight of him in his dark suit and white button-down shirt put her in a trance.

Kendall beamed up at Luke. "Hi," she said as he walked in and kissed her. She tingled all the way down to her toes. The way he kissed her set her core on fire.

He stepped back and held up a brown paper bag with his right hand. "I brought dinner."

"Great, thank you."

"I'll set it in the kitchen."

"Perfect. I opened a bottle of red earlier. If you'd like, I'll pour you a glass."

He glanced over his shoulder and gave her a devilish smile. "Yes, please."

Kendall strolled into the kitchen with a goofy grin. She grabbed a glass from the cabinet and filled it with the crimson liquid and topped off her glass too. She leaned against the counter, sipping, as she watched Luke fiddle with the knobs on the oven in what looked like an attempt to figure out how to warm dinner. He cocked his head and shut the oven door.

Turning around, after finally getting the oven to work, he headed toward her. "Rough day, huh?"

She nodded. "I never thought I'd be questioned in a murder investigation. You should've heard them, Luke. I swear, they think I did it. They think I'm a murderer! How did my life go from normal a year ago—boring even—to a widowed murder suspect? It feels unreal, like I'm living in a bad dream."

Luke furrowed his brows. "Do you really think you're a suspect?"

"You should've seen Gates. My God, if I didn't know better, I'd say he was convinced I'm guilty. The way he looked at me, it was different, not like before." She shook her head in frustration.

She felt betrayed by both Marcus and Detective Gates. Marcus had always been sweet and comforting since the whole nightmare began. Now, he was stone cold, as if they'd never met.

"Well, you know, typically in a murder investigation, they always look at the spouse first. They're probably just following protocol. Maybe they're going hard at you to clear you fast in order to move on to the real killer." He paused and stepped back. "You didn't do it, right?"

Kendall flinched at the accusation. Was he serious? "Of course not."

He moved closer to her and put his hands around her waist, gently pulling her glass down and placing it on the counter. Braiding his fingers between hers, he pulled her closer, pressing his warm body to hers. "Good. I'd hate to think I've fallen for a femme fatale."

Kendall smiled wide. "You've fallen for me?" Was what she felt real? It surely felt that way.

He lowered his face to hers. "Absolutely." He leaned in until their lips met. He kissed her soft and slow, and she bit his lower lip, letting him know she wanted more than a "sweet gesture." She was hungry, and not for what was in the oven. Kendall increased the intensity of her probing before moving her hands down his neck and resting them on his broad shoulders.

Luke slid his hands up her rib cage, stopping to explore her chest. She thought she would melt into a puddle right there on the kitchen floor.

He slid his hands back down and up her blouse, unhooking her bra. She momentarily let go of him to pull her shirt over her head and threw it on the floor, along with her black lace bra. He tugged her closer and then kissed her hard on the mouth before slowly descending his lips down her neck to her shoulder. He lifted her up on the counter and sat her next to his glass of untouched wine. He kissed her on the mouth, hungrily, before continuing down her neck and further south. She let out a gasp, and he moved his right hand to unbutton her jeans. Her body was on fire. He tucked his hand into her waistband and wrapped it around her right hip. And then he froze.

Breathlessly, she said, "What's wrong?"

He pulled back and took several deep breaths, not meeting her gaze. "Not here. Not like this."

She didn't know what to say. What was wrong with here and now? He released her and picked up her blouse and bra from the kitchen floor, handing them to her. She accepted them —silently.

His eyes bore into hers. "I want this badly. There aren't enough words to describe how much I want you, Kendall. But, I want to start this off right—not like . . ."

Kendall slid her shirt over her head and descended from the counter. "Like what?"

He met her gaze. "Like before. When we saw each other before, it was mostly sex and that's not what I'm after here. I want more. I want to do this right."

Kendall felt as if the air had been knocked out of her. It hadn't been just sex for her, but she hadn't told him that, all those years ago.

She wiped the sweat from her brow. "Okay, so what does that mean?"

With sincere eyes, pleading with her, he said, "I want to wait to, *you know*, until we're having an amazingly, romantic date and not a response to a bad day."

She didn't want him because of a bad day. She wanted him because she'd wanted him for more than a decade. She stared at him. "I guess I understand, but for the record, I don't want you because of a bad day. I want you, because I want *you*. But I'm okay with waiting for a more romantic scenario." She attempted a reassuring smile. She wasn't sure what would be more romantic, but she hoped Luke planned something soon, because when she was with him, her logic shut down and her desire took over. She simply couldn't resist him.

"You're really okay with waiting?"

No. "Yes, of course." When in her life had a man ever wanted to wait? She supposed there was a first time for everything.

"Okay, then if you want me to stay for dinner, I suggest you put on your bra, because I can see your nipples through that shirt of yours. And I am gonna need a distraction. Maybe we can watch a movie with wrinkly old people in it? And absolutely no love scenes."

She laughed as he continued on about all the things they couldn't watch. It was sweet, and it was funny, and he was adorable. But a large part of her wished he'd change his mind.

She smiled. "Wrinkly old people it is."

He placed her hands in his and said, "Thank you."

"For what?"

"For being you. For being with me. For making me the happiest man, near happiest, *that* will come later."

She was sure she turned fifty shades of pink. Maybe this was time for a bit of clarity? "So, I'm just going to ask this. I think I know the answer, but . . . are you dating other people? Do you want to date other people?"

He shook his head. "One hundred percent no. You are the only one I want. That I'll ever want."

Ever? "Oh." She wasn't sure what to make of that.

His eyes widened. "And you?"

"Oh, I'm not seeing anyone else. And, I don't want to."

He pulled her close. "Does that mean you'll be my girlfriend?"

"Are you asking me to be your girlfriend?" she repeated.

He nodded.

"Yes."

He kissed her gently and pulled back. "Perfect. Now stop trying to seduce me."

She laughed as he released her to check on their dinner. She had a "boyfriend." *And* she was a person of interest in a murder investigation. Luke had almost made her forget. *Almost.*

CHAPTER NINETEEN

MARCUS

Marcus added Luke Abbington's name to the board under the short list of potential suspects. He stepped back. *And then there were three*, he thought. They were nearly certain that Irwin Dratch had been hired to kill George Davis. There was no link whatsoever between Irwin Dratch and George Davis. Nor was there a motive for Dratch to kill George. Unfortunately for them, Dratch still wasn't talking. He wasn't talking to police, other inmates, or any visitors. According to the corrections facility, the only person he spoke to was his lawyer.

Why would Dratch keep the person who had hired him a secret? Honor among thieves? Without Dratch's cooperation, they had no concrete evidence against anyone. But Dratch was the one doing the time, so why wouldn't he talk? Did he think he stood a better chance in court?

Having just returned from interrogation, Marcus watched Luke leave the station. Was Luke sweating? Nobody sweats in the cold interview room, unless they have a reason to.

Marcus studied the board next to his desk. First in the line of unofficial suspects was Kendall Murphy, wife of the deceased. There didn't appear to be a financial motive, and they hadn't found any connection between her and Irwin Dratch. Nor had they proven she had any extramarital affairs, and therefore, she didn't appear to have a motive. However, the mention of Luke Abbington in the interview did shed light on their latest person of interest.

Marcus was shocked, as was Gates: Luke Abbington confessed that he and Kendall had only been dating for the last month, but he'd been in love with Kendall for the last ten years. That's a long time to be in love with someone. And coincidentally, both murder suspects' spouses had died. Had Luke and Kendall just happened to bump into one another on the street?

Gates approached the murder board, pointing at the dark-haired suspect. "Yeah, if I was a betting man, I'd bet on Luke Abbington for this."

"What's your theory?" Marcus hoped it didn't implicate Kendall. He was tired of chasing the Kendall theory. He knew in his gut she hadn't murdered her husband.

"Well, the fact he's been in love with her for the last ten years raises a red flag. But my theory is: after Luke's wife died tragically of cancer two years ago, he snapped. He snapped and decided that it was finally his time with Kendall, but there's only one problem, she's married. All he has to do to have Kendall in his life is to get rid of George Davis. Luke's financials aren't back yet, but I'm guessing he's got plenty of money to hire a top-notch hitman. No question."

Marcus thought about what Gates had said. It did seem to fit. Tragedy and heartbreak, such as the death of a spouse, could do things to a man. Perhaps Luke did have some sort of psychological break and decided he'd have Kendall at any cost. Marcus said, "Okay. I say that's a fairly reasonable theory. So, next we get a full list of his financials, full background, and look for any connection between Irwin Dratch and Luke Abbington. We should be able to get cell phone records too."

Gates leaned against the desk. "Most definitely, and not just Luke Abbington's. We need Kendall Murphy's records as well. We'll have to get a warrant." He eyed Marcus. "There are a couple more theories for these two lovers. Theory number one: Luke acted alone. Wife dies, he snaps and decides Kendall is to be his and boom, takes out George Davis. Theory number two: Kendall decided she wanted her husband's fortune and takes him out. Theory number three: Kendall and Luke were having an affair, and Kendall decides she wants Luke, free and clear, and hires Dratch to kill her husband. Theory number four: they were seeing one another, prior to George's death, and they conspired together."

Acted together? Marcus had a hard time believing that Kendall was a homicidal mastermind in cahoots with this Luke Abbington. He shook his head, not buying it for a second. Despite the mounting motive, he said, "Or theory five: none of the above. We still haven't talked to his family. What if the brother had something to do with it? After all, he's the one stuck at home, taking care of Mother, while George planned a wonderful, carefree life with Kendall."

"Buddy, you're right. We need to take a road trip to Bakersfield and get statements from the family. Maybe there's something we haven't looked at yet, although my money is still on Luke and maybe Kendall."

Marcus leaned back against his desk, crossing his arms. He agreed, but felt there were major pieces of the puzzle still missing. And he hoped the pieces would fall into place once they received the background information on Luke.

If they didn't find something concrete soon, the odds of finding the person or persons who hired Dratch plummeted. Marcus was beyond frustrated. So far, all their theories were just theories. They hadn't proven anything, other than Irwin Dratch was the one to actually do the deed. Did Luke Abbington hire Irwin Dratch to kill George Davis? Did Kendall have her husband taken out? Or was his brother involved? Marcus's head spun from the possibilities. For a case he wanted so badly to solve, he thought it would've been done by now.

CHAPTER TWENTY

LUKE

LUKE SAT IN HIS CAR AND POUNDED ON THE STEERING wheel. How had he let it slip that he'd been in love with Kendall for the last ten years? Stupid. Stupid. Stupid. Reckless moron! He hadn't even told Kendall his true feelings.

He lowered his hands and breathed heavily. He wasn't a moron, but he might be one of the top suspects now. Jesus, this had gone all wrong. He wanted every part of his relationship with Kendall to be perfect. And now they were both murder suspects. Boy, had he screwed that up. He started the car and commanded the voice activation system. "Call Kendall Murphy." The car replied, "Calling Kendall Murphy cell phone."

Kendall answered cheerfully. "Hey there." Her voice soothed him, simmering him down.

"How are you?"

"I'm all right, I just got home from work, and this place is still a disaster. I think I'll start packing up, maybe stay in a hotel this weekend—it's just too chaotic here, plus it needs to be finished by Monday so they can start staging the place for the market."

"Stay in a hotel?"

"Yeah, Janine got me thinking, since she's moving out, while the house is for sale, I'll stay at a hotel. I could use a change of scenery. It'll be like a mini-vacation, and who doesn't love in-room dining and maid service?"

As much as he wanted to talk about her mini-vacation, or maybe invite her to stay with him, he couldn't overlook what had just taken place. "I'm calling to let you know I'm leaving the police station."

"What? The police station. Why were you there?" Her previously carefree voice was now riddled with worry.

"The detectives came to my office today and asked that I come down to answer questions. I assumed it wouldn't be a problem and simply wanted to get it over with."

"I'm so sorry, Luke. I hate that you got dragged into this. The whole thing is awful."

"Unfortunately, it gets a bit worse, but I think we should talk in person. Anyway, want to come over to my place tonight? I can pick you up. I'm not far away."

A ruffling noise muffled the call, as if Kendall lowered the phone from her ear. Was she hesitating? Why? Then the noise cleared, and she said, "I suppose I could clean up tomorrow."

"I'll see you in a little bit."

Luke ended the call. This wasn't going according to plan. He'd have to explain to Kendall why he was now a likely murder suspect. He'd never wanted to tell her that he'd been thinking of her all these years, assuming they could start fresh. But we don't always get what we want. *Isn't that the truth?* Still, he hoped that wasn't true of Kendall. He wanted her more than he'd ever wanted anything in his life.

Luke sat next to Kendall on his sofa, facing her. She looked at him with eager eyes. What was she thinking? Did he see love in her eyes? He peered closer. Looking at her was like a warm coat that he never wanted to take off. He rested his hand on her thigh. She sipped her wine and then drained her glass. Setting it down on the glass-top coffee table, it landed with a clank. "What's wrong? Was the interview awful?" she asked.

It's now or never, Luke thought. "I told the detective something I hadn't planned to say, and this isn't how I wanted to tell you, but it's important for you to know, because I bet I'm now at the top of their suspect list for George's murder."

Kendall's eyes widened, and she sat back. "What do you mean? How are you a suspect? I don't understand."

"Kendall, this is hard to say." He paused. "They were asking about my relationship with you and about our history. I explained about us having worked together, and then they asked if I ever had feelings for you back then. I didn't want to lie, so I told them yes."

Kendall grabbed his hand on her leg. "That's not so bad, right? It was a long time ago. Why would it be relevant now? Maybe you're overreacting—this whole thing is so crazy. I doubt you're a real suspect."

Luke carefully shut his eyes and breathed before opening them again. "There's more." He reached over and drained his glass of wine as well. "They asked how strong those feelings were, and if I had ever stopped having those feelings for you. And I suppose I paused too long, because then they fired away with accusations. I lost my composure." He swallowed. "Not one of my finer moments." He put his other hand on Kendall's leg. He tried to tell her, but he was having trouble with the right words. What if she thought he was a psycho? Or a stalker? Or responsible for George's murder? He never wanted to tell her this way. He hadn't wanted to tell her at all.

He averted his eyes, staring down at his hands on her thighs. *Now or never, Luke.* "I confessed to being in love with you, and that those feelings had never gone away." Luke braced himself as he glanced up at her.

Kendall's mouth dropped open. He watched as her attention fluttered around the room, clearly contemplating his admission. He prayed this wouldn't be the end of them. He didn't know what he'd do if he lost her too.

She stared at him, with pain in her eyes. "I don't know what to say. We never talked about it before."

It was how Luke had wanted it. He didn't want to remind her, or himself, of the abrupt ending to their too-short relationship. He had deep feelings for Kendall back then, but hadn't realized it was love until it was too late. Grace had begged him to give their marriage one more try, and as much as he had thought it was over, he felt he owed it to Grace and his marriage to give it another shot. They had exchanged vows, and those vows meant something to him. It wasn't until he'd gone back to his old life, one without Kendall, that he realized his true feelings for her.

His heart pounded. "Kendall, this isn't how I wanted to tell you. I wanted us to start fresh. I didn't want to seem like some maniac who'd been holding a torch all these years, but please know that I do. I love you."

She still hadn't said she loved him back. Had he been wrong? He thought he could feel her love. But maybe it'd been wishful thinking. Maybe she wasn't ready for love.

Kendall sat up straight and gazed into his eyes. They sparkled like giant emeralds. "Luke, I know it sounds crazy, but . . . I love you, too."

He knew it. Kendall was his. He wrapped his arms around her and pulled her in, kissing her passionately. He could kiss her all day and all night, but there were other parts of her he'd yet to taste. He wanted to taste them all. Heart pounding, he slowly backed away, "Would you like to move this into the bedroom?"

She gazed at him with fire in her eyes. "Absolutely."

He took her by the hand and led her into his bedroom.

LUKE LAY IN BED AS KENDALL RETURNED FROM THE bathroom, wearing nothing but a coy smile. With tussled hair and flushed cheeks, she had never looked more beautiful. She climbed into bed and curled up next to him before draping her arm across his chest. He lowered his lips to meet hers. He said, "I love you."

"I love you, too."

He knew at that moment he could die and he'd die happy.

He kissed her sweetly. "What were you saying earlier about staying at a hotel?"

She backed off him and propped herself up on her side. "Yeah, with Janine moving out, and the house going on the market next week, I thought it would be nice to have a change of scenery. I figured a hotel was a logical option while I find something more permanent."

He placed his hand on her hip and tugged her closer. "Why don't you stay here, with me?"

"Are you serious? This is . . . I don't know, too soon?"

"It doesn't necessarily have to be permanent. It can be your change of scenery while you look for a new place. You can call it Hotel Abbington. I'll make you dinner, and I'll even up my maid service if you'd like it to have a more hotel-like feel. What do you say?"

She didn't answer for a while. Had he gone too far? It was too much too soon. She looked back up at him. "Can I think about it?"

He squeezed her tighter. “Of course.” Luke didn’t mind that she needed to think about it. She could have as much time as she wanted. He wasn’t going anywhere.

CHAPTER TWENTY-ONE

KENDALL

On her drive home from work, Kendall replayed the morning and previous night in her head. Waking up in Luke's arms felt so natural, so necessary, so warm. She'd half expected to feel guilty, as if it were a betrayal to George, but she hadn't. She knew George would want her to be happy, and of course, if the situation had been reversed, she'd have wanted George to be happy with another woman.

Should she move in with Luke? What were the implications if she did? What if they lived together and he decided that he didn't want her there after all? It would be like a kick in the teeth if she got booted out by her new boyfriend. It was all moving so fast. Within the span of a month, she and Luke had started dating, they'd slept together, and now they were potentially moving in together. At this rate, they'd be married by the end of the year. She envisioned standing next to him in an off-white gown with a silly grin on her face as he smiled back at her.

Wow, Kendall. Yikes. Too soon. With those wacky thoughts floating around, she knew it was too soon to be cohabiting. She obviously wasn't thinking clearly. No, there was far too much going on for Luke and her to take that big of a step.

Moving. Selling the house. Not to mention the investigation into George's death. How long would it be before the police cleared her name? When could she move on? They had absolutely no evidence, it was absurd that she was even a suspect. And Luke was now a suspect. It wasn't possible that Luke could have killed George, was it?

Before she contemplated such a large question, she slammed on her breaks, nearly ramming into the car in front of her. Her mouth dropped open at the sight of six news vans and news crews milling about outside her house. The scene was more hectic than the trading floor at the New York Stock Exchange. People were *everywhere.*

What was happening? A glimmer of hope ignited within her. Had they found out who hired Irwin Dratch to kill her husband? Were they there for her to comment on how she felt about the killer? Why hadn't the detectives called her?

She grabbed for the remote to open the garage, but remembered her garage was filled with moving boxes. *Dammit.* She inched up her driveway, trying not to add felony vehicular manslaughter to her list of charges. She continued slowly up the driveway and the reporters moved back. As she set the car into park, reporters swarmed around her like bees to honey.

She grabbed her laptop case, threw it over her shoulder, opened the door, and stepped out of her car. Before she could even shut the door behind her, one reporter shoved a black microphone into her face. The woman, wearing far too much make-up, asked, "Kendall Murphy, is it true that you hired a hitman to kill your husband?"

Kendall's mouth dropped open. "What?" Stunned, she could barely move. She shook her head and tried to regain her composure and function in order to move forward, out of the spotlight. As she pushed past the reporters, they continued to shout out questions.

"Is it true you and Luke Abbington have been engaged in an affair for over a decade and plotted to kill each other's spouses?"

"Did you act alone?"

"Did you do it for money?"

"Did you know Luke killed your husband?"

Kendall rushed to her front door, dodging reporters' elbows and microphones and fumbling with her keys as she tried to unlock the front door.

Inside, she had to use her back to close the door and keep the insects at bay. Her heart raced as she leaned against the door, locking it. What was happening? Who had leaked to the press that she and Luke were suspects in George's murder? How on earth had all this gone from so very bad to so very worse?

Would her face be splashed across all the news channels? What the hell was she supposed to do in this situation? She threw her bag down on the sofa and paced around her living room. She told herself, "Calm down. Think. You need to call Janine and the lawyer."

She pulled her phone from her laptop bag and selected her sister from the list of favorites. "Hey, Janine, it's me. There are reporters surrounding the house, I don't think it's safe for you to be here. I don't know what happened—but they think I killed George. It's awful. If you have somewhere else you can stay tonight, you might want to think about it. If not, we can get you a hotel room."

"Oh my God! Are you sure you don't want me to be there with you?"

"I don't think it's safe. I'm about to call my lawyer and ask her what to do. This is so fucking bizarre."

"I can crash with a friend. Where are you going to stay?"

"Probably a hotel, if I can get out of here without being

harassed. I need to talk to Cybil. I'll call you after I find out more, okay?"

"Okay. Be safe."

Kendall scrolled through her contacts for Cybil Hernandez's information. She thought hiring Cybil had just been a formality. Now she had reporters on her doorstep. She found the number and dialed. Taking deep breaths, she waited for the receptionist to answer. "Hernandez, Jones & McIntyre. How may I help you?"

"Hi, my name is Kendall Murphy. I'm a client of Cybil Hernandez, and I need to talk to her. I've got reporters outside my home and I don't know what to do."

The receptionist said, "I'll get her right away. Please hold."

Kendall continued to pace the length of her living room.

"Kendall?"

"Yes, Cybil, this is Kendall."

"The receptionist said there are reporters at your house. Tell me what's happening."

Kendall described the scene, peeking out the edge of a curtain. A camera flash went off outside and she jerked away from the limelight.

"I'm so sorry this is happening. Let me put in a call to some friends at City Hall to figure out how the story got leaked and why. I have a feeling they may be doing this to put pressure on you and Luke to get one of you to break. Sit tight, and I'll come to you. We'll go over a plan to keep you safe and out of the press. Don't open the door for anyone but me. Give me an hour."

"Okay, thanks."

Kendall tucked her phone in her back pocket and jetted upstairs to pack a bag.

A KNOCK ON THE DOOR WAS FOLLOWED BY A MUFFLED shout. "Kendall, it's me, Cybil!"

Kendall rushed over to the front door to quickly open it and then slammed it closed behind Cybil. Cybil embraced her with a hug. "It's like a zoo out there. You would think after an hour they would've gone home by now."

"Thank you so much for coming. I'm not sure what I'm supposed to do."

"I talked to my contact at City Hall. There was definitely a leak to the press. They think a warrant for both yours and Luke's cell phone records was the trigger. The leak likely came from someone who was part of that warrant-issuing process. It's now in the media that the two of you are potential suspects, but of course, they have it slanted that you are suspects not potential suspects. We'll get you somewhere safe, but I think maybe it's time you walk me through the whole Luke situation —from the beginning to where you are right now. It's important."

"The Luke situation?"

"When did your relationship start? How did it start? How serious is it now? And most importantly, why do they think he's a suspect?"

Kendall nodded. She explained Luke's confession to the police and how they had confessed their love for one another the previous night.

Cybil jotted some notes down on her yellow legal pad. She said, "I need to ask you some questions that may seem harsh and intrusive, but that the police are likely to ask you as well. Know that I am asking this is as your lawyer, as someone who needs all the facts to properly defend you. Okay?"

Kendall nodded.

"Did you know Luke had feelings for you all this time?"

She shook her head. "No, I didn't know." She had been

shocked by his confession the previous evening. It was the best surprise she'd received in a long time.

"So the two of you never had a romantic relationship?"

"Not exactly." Kendall explained their brief affair and her quick departure from the company shortly after it had ended. "I hadn't seen or talked to him in ten years, until I ran into him at Aqua Restaurant, the day of George's funeral. I ran into him again, about six months later, the day of Janine's graduation."

Cybil cocked her head. "So, you never had contact with him while George was alive?"

"No. Never."

"So, what you're saying is you didn't see or speak to Luke for ten years, but since your husband's death, you ran into him accidentally—twice?"

Kendall didn't like the air quotes Cybil put around the word "ran," but she let that question sink in. Was Cybil implying that maybe their meet-ups weren't coincidental? Was she implying that Luke may have had George killed?

Kendall nodded. "That's correct. I hadn't seen him in ten years and then saw him twice. The second time is when he asked me to meet for coffee. We've been seeing a lot of each other since then, and then last night, we told each other how we felt."

Cybil licked her lips. "Hmm. Did you share this ten-year love with him? Basically, what I'm asking is, do you feel the same about Luke as he does about you?"

"It wasn't that I was pining away for him for the last decade, but he was always in the back of my mind. I loved George, I did, but there was always a piece of Luke inside of me. It's hard to explain. Anyway, I thought that ship had sailed and didn't give a relationship with him a second thought. Until now."

Cybil remained stoic. "And you had absolutely no contact with him in the last ten years, before you ran into him after

George's death? No calls. No emails. No bumping into each other at a conference . . ."

"None."

"The first time you ran into him, had Luke been aware that George had died?"

"Yes, but that's not strange. Luke works at George's company. There had to be some sort of notice at work."

"Sounds reasonable. But I'm going to be frank with you, your involvement with Luke makes you look guilty. In today's world, with social media and the press, the appearance of guilt and public opinion goes pretty far in a case like this. This is a quiet, upper-middle-class neighborhood; not a lot of bad things happen here. But a man was murdered, a 'murder for hire' no less, and it heightens the sensationalism around it. From the outside looking in, it looks like the widow, who the press says is involved in her husband's murder, is now dating the long-lost love, also accused of the murder. Being seen with Luke is bad for you. Professionally, personally, and in court."

Kendall blinked furiously. "Do you think I'll be arrested and this will go to trial?"

"It depends. If they can't find anything linking you to Luke before George's death, they won't have a motive for you to have killed George, and likely, you'll be cleared. But, if they're convinced you or Luke were involved, they may arrest you, and it could very well go to trial. As of right now, there's no evidence against you, and if what you say is true, there won't be any. It doesn't mean the press won't make your life a living hell until they arrest the actual person responsible for hiring Dratch."

"What am I supposed to do? I can't just wait around as the world thinks I've killed my husband and had some torrid affair with my coconspirator."

"We need to hire a private investigator and try to find another suspect. It'll provide reasonable doubt for you, and we may even discover who killed your husband. Private investigators can do things the police are restricted from doing. I think it's our best bet. You'll need a damn good private investigator to get this resolved as quickly as possible. I have someone in mind, but I have to warn you, it's not going to be cheap."

Kendall didn't care about the money. She just wanted all of the chaos to stop and to find justice for George. If none of this had happened, she'd probably be hanging out, reading a book about what to expect when you're expecting. A wave of sadness washed over her. *Life rarely turns out the way you expect it to. Best laid plans and all.*

"Money isn't an issue."

"Let me rephrase when I say expensive. I mean it could go into the six figures."

Kendall's eyes widened. "Six figures?" She paused. "I can make it work."

"Great. The next step will be to move you somewhere where the press can't get to you. Do you have anywhere to go?"

Kendall remembered Luke's offer. "Luke recently offered to let me stay with him as I was looking for a new place but . . ."

Cybil raised her hands in the air. "Absolutely not. I cannot stress this enough. You cannot move into Luke's place. Also, it would be in your best interest if you stay away from Luke—at least until we clear your name."

Kendall let that sink in. Not see Luke. The vortex kept on spinning, sucking her down even further. It was a bottomless pit of bad news. "Well, I had contemplated staying at a hotel near work, in San Francisco, while the house is up for sale, until I found a new place. It was then that Luke offered for me to stay with him. Which I won't, obviously."

"I think a hotel is a great idea. You should check in today. I'll book the hotel under the name of one of my associates so the press can't find you. You'll want to either work from the hotel or take some vacation days. The bloodsuckers aren't likely to walk away until this is solved, or a bigger story makes the headlines."

Kendall hoped for the former and wasn't sure what to say. "I packed earlier. So, I'm ready to go."

"Perfect. Give me a minute."

Kendall watched as Cybil walked toward the door and spoke on the phone. She wondered when the nightmare would end.

Cybil returned. "Reservation is made. I'll take you in my car to a café, so we can lose the press if they try to follow. And then we'll get you settled into the hotel."

Kendall was overwhelmed with gratitude for Beth, who had suggested hiring a lawyer. What would she have done if she didn't have a lawyer? She would've been eaten alive.

Before she got up from the dining table, Cybil asked, "Have you talked to Luke since you've been home?"

"I called him after I talked to you. He said that nobody had approached him from the press, and he wanted to come over, but I said I'd talk to him when I knew my plans."

"You guys shouldn't be seen in public."

Kendall's heart sank. That morning, she was wrapped in Luke's arms, safe from the world around them. He'd almost made her believe in happy endings again. *Almost.*

CHAPTER TWENTY-TWO

KENDALL

DESPITE THE FACT THAT SHE WAS IN SNEAKERS AND JEANS, Kendall struggled to keep up with Cybil, who wore three-inch heels and a pencil skirt. It was dizzying how quickly Cybil had thrown together Kendall's incognito plan.

After they had left the house, Cybil had navigated past the reporters, losing them after they followed suit. Then they exchanged cars with one of her associates and she handed Kendall a disguise. They made it to her hotel in the Financial District, without the press catching on to her location in San Francisco. Cybil Hernandez was a formidable woman. There was no question. Kendall stood behind Cybil at the counter as she was checked in under an alias.

On the way to the bank of elevators, up to her new home away from home, Kendall adjusted her blonde wig and baseball cap. Cybil stepped into an elevator and held the door open with her arm.

"I'll bring you up to the room and review the plan for the next couple days, in order to keep you safe and out of the media. Hopefully, this will all be over very soon. How are you holding up?"

Kendall shrugged. "I'm kind of still taking it all in."

"Well, I think you're doing admirably."

The ding of the elevator indicated they'd arrived on their floor. Kendall stepped out and headed toward the room with the key card in hand.

She lugged her suitcase in as Cybil shut the door behind them. Kendall sat on the edge of one of the queen-sized beds while Cybil immediately set up shop on the desk in the corner of the hotel room.

"Can I leave the hotel?" Kendall asked.

"If you hide your hair well, that should help, but it's not a foolproof plan. Even with your disguise, someone may still be able to identify you."

It would be nice if she could blend in better, but alas that was not her fate. Kendall had received comments on her reddish-auburn hair and bright-green eyes ever since childhood; it was the Irish heritage. Her grandmother had assured her it was because she'd been blessed with the luck of the Irish. She wasn't feeling that luck at the moment.

"No visitors either?"

"Not Luke, obviously. And your sister . . . someone may see her and put two and two together. I hate to have to isolate you, but I think it's the best approach at this time."

Kendall shifted on the bed. No Luke. No Janine. Maybe Beth? "What if I had a friend come and visit, like my friend Beth? She has a unique look, but she lives here in San Francisco, so she could be visiting anyone."

"Beth should be okay, but let me have her cleared first."

Jeez. Only cleared persons can visit?

"Try to stay in the room for the next couple of days. Also, you may want to wear the hat and wig when room service delivers food. Or if you have Beth visit, have her bring food or answer the door. Next, we need to address the fact that any calls you make from now on can and most likely will be made public to the police. As we discussed, you need to limit all communications with Luke." Cybil raised her right hand. It stopped Kendall from protesting. It was as if Cybil knew exactly what Kendall was about to say.

"Everything you do, Kendall, is your choice. But this is your life. In my opinion, if Luke means this much to you, a few days or weeks without contact shouldn't affect your relationship, but I can't force you to do anything. As your lawyer, I can advise you on what I think is the best course of action and the most likely way to keep you out of the press and out of jail."

She knew that Cybil was right. Maybe some alone time was what she needed anyhow. It'd give her time to think about her plans instead of just letting things happen *to* her. Sure, she was sequestered in a hotel room, but that didn't mean she couldn't do anything. Aside from meeting with clients, her entire job could be done online. It's the digital age and all. You can do practically everything online. No, she'd jump into work and take this time to come up with a plan to take her life back—assuming she'd get it back.

Cybil studied the screen on her laptop. "Okay, so we're clear on limiting communications with non-necessary people in your life to keep you safe. Next, I'll have you meet with my private investigator so she can go over some of the details of what her team will be looking at in order to get this moving as fast as humanly possible. She'll drop by tomorrow to speak with you."

A female investigator? For some reason Kendall has assumed the investigator would be male. Hearing that she was female eased her angst a bit. "Okay." Would Kendall be allowed to help with the investigation? After George's death, she had felt so helpless, like a victim, and she didn't like it. She wanted to do something. *Anything.*

"Do you have any questions? If not, I'll send you the details for my PI, Selena Bailey. She'll be contacting you for the meeting and to obtain some preliminary details on the case. I have to warn you, Selena can be a bit . . . intense, but she's one of the best in her field. We were lucky to hire her on such short notice. If you have any questions at all, call me or Selena, anytime."

How intense? "No questions for now. Thank you for everything. I don't know what I would've done if I hadn't found you when I did."

Cybil stood up. "All in a day's work. We'll get you through this."

Before she shut the door as her lawyer left, Cybil swiveled around. "One more thing. I would avoid watching the news."

Kendall hadn't even contemplated watching the news. However, now she wanted to. She nodded and waved. "Have a good night."

"Take care."

Kendall shut the door.

Clicking on the television to the first news channel she could find, the first station featured the weather and warned of an impending heatwave in the Bay Area. Not so bad. She clicked to the next news channel, and her mouth dropped open. Her photo was splashed across the screen with a too-chipper newscaster describing the allegations against her and Luke. Luke's photo was then brought up on the screen next to hers. The newscaster called them the "killer couple." Kendall was about to be physically ill.

Glued to where she stood in front of the flat screen, she felt like she was having an out-of-body experience as she watched someone who looked exactly like her, exiting her car outside her home. Up in the right corner, a photo of George was displayed. Her heart skipped a beat. They kept referring to him as "the victim, George Davis."

She rushed to the bathroom and vomited the contents of her cafe dinner into the toilet. Kendall sat on the cold tile floor and cried. She cried for George. She cried for her old life. She cried for her crying on the bathroom floor. After the sob session, a jolt of realization shot through her. She wanted her old life back, and she knew at that moment that she would have given anything to press rewind on the last year and be at home, safe in her bed, lying next to George.

Guilt spiked through her.

What about Luke? She thought she loved him. But was it real or just her memory of how she had loved him before? There was no denying the chemistry they shared, but they hardly knew one another. Ten years was a long time to not be in someone's life. Why did it feel so real? Maybe she had hoped it was? At that moment, if she had to choose between Luke and George, she would choose George, without hesitation. What did that mean? Why had she told Luke she loved him if she wasn't ready? Could her life be more of a disaster?

She told herself to get a grip, and using the bathtub as a crutch, she hoisted herself off the floor. She zombie-walked to the sink and stared in the mirror. A pink, puffy mess stared back at her. She flicked on the faucet and splashed cool water on her face, until she no longer tasted the salt from her tears.

She looked around the beige hotel room, holding her stomach. In one big room, there were two queen beds, a love seat, a coffee table, and a desk. This would be her home for the foreseeable future. No George. No Luke. No one but herself.

She picked up her cell phone from the bed and paused. Luke was calling. She squeezed her eyes shut, unsure if she wanted to talk to him right now. She ignored it, and instead, called Janine to let her know the current situation.

Hanging up, her phone buzzed again. *Luke.* She couldn't avoid him forever. What about just for the rest of the day? She shook her head, realizing he might go to her house if she didn't answer. Time to be brave. She answered, "Hi."

"I haven't heard from you in hours. Are you okay? People are calling me left and right."

The sound of his voice and obvious love warmed her insides. Why was this so confusing? Faced with telling him they wouldn't be seeing or talking to one another for the foreseeable future, she wasn't sure she had the heart to do it. "I'm fine. I'm staying at a hotel under a false name, and I shouldn't say more, but Luke, there's something I have to tell you."

"What is it, honey?"

Honey. George had always called her honey. Never sweetheart or darling. Just honey.

She shut her eyes. "I've been advised to cut off contact with you, at least until this is all sorted out. That includes no talking on the phone or seeing each other in person. With the media and allegations, the visual is bad for me and for you."

"But the allegations are nonsense. I didn't do this. You didn't do this. We didn't do anything wrong. I don't agree with this approach at all, Kendall. I know your lawyer has a good reputation, but I'm not sure about this particular advice. I think we're stronger together than we are apart."

She knew she needed to go with the advice from her lawyer, and she also needed some space. Cybil was right; if she and Luke were meant to be, a little time apart shouldn't harm anything. If it did, it wasn't meant to be. "I'm sorry, but I think it's best too. This is all so crazy, and I need your support on this. We shouldn't be seen together—it looks bad, you know that."

"But . . ." his voice fell silent.

She squeezed the phone, wishing he was more cooperative. If he continued, this would be their first official argument, and she couldn't deal with it, not now. Not when she was simply trying to survive.

"You're right. I apologize. I'll respect your wishes. Hopefully, this is settled soon. I miss you."

"I miss you, too." She did. She missed how when she was with him, the rest of the world faded away.

"I understand not being seen together, but no phone calls either? How will I know you're all right?"

"I don't know. I just need to take my lawyer's advice. We can't communicate with one another for now. As soon as I can, I'll call you, okay? That means no texting either." She held her breath as she waited for his response. And she waited. "Luke?"

"I'm here. I don't know what else to say."

Kendall's heart sunk into her chest. She'd already lost George. Now it seemed she may lose Luke too.

CHAPTER TWENTY-THREE

LUKE

Luke slammed his phone down onto the table. Rage filled his core. He couldn't believe how stupid he'd been. If he'd kept his mouth shut and never told the police his true feelings about Kendall, the two of them wouldn't be in this situation. He wouldn't be a murder suspect, and he wouldn't be cut off from Kendall. Not to mention what the press would do to his reputation. Would his clients back out? Could he be fired from Stickman Capital? He needed to think through all of this rationally. He couldn't lose her—or his reputation.

Her love was what brought him back to life after so much grief and so much loneliness. She was his future, and he knew that in his soul. She'd left a permanent mark on him, one that could never be removed. He would stop at nothing to make sure they were together for good. He stared down at the oak table where he had slammed down his phone. He needed to resolve this, and quickly. He needed to talk to his lawyer, but with the day nearing midnight, it would have to wait until morning.

How long could he go without talking to Kendall or feeling her soft body against his? Now that he'd had a taste, there was no way he could have anything else. Whatever it took, even if he had to hire a team of lawyers, it didn't matter. He *needed* to be with her.

"DAVE, I KNOW YOU'RE THE TOP OF YOUR FIELD, BUT HOW bad is it to be seen with Kendall right now? I can't even talk to her on the phone. They don't have a wiretap, right?"

Through the phone, his lawyer explained, "You being seen with Kendall is like Jeffrey Dahmer walking around with a severed head in his hands. It's that bad. Luke, Kendall has a damn good lawyer. That lawyer will be investigating and tearing apart everybody's life in order to clear Kendall. She's not going to consider your feelings or your life. Right now, you need to protect yourself so that you don't end up in prison. So, if you want my advice, here it is: you need to stay away from Kendall until this is all cleared up. Don't call her. Don't text her. Don't email her. No contact with her. If you want to stay out of jail and out of the press, you'll follow my advice."

Luke shook his head in anger. He couldn't believe his lawyer was agreeing with Kendall's.

Was he blinded by his feelings for her? Considering he was paying Dave a lot of money for his legal advice, Luke didn't question him. "Okay. I've got it. What do we do next to clear our names? I assume hire a team of investigators to get to the bottom of it. I don't care what it costs, but I want it done fast."

"I hear you. We can do all of that. I've got the names of some people. If the information can be found, it will be found. It will cost you, but you said money is no object, so we'll get it done. Luke, I need to warn you that in order to find George's killer, we'll have to tear apart not only George and Kendall's life, but yours as well. If you have any skeletons, they're coming out."

Luke figured as much. He was mostly clean. But *mostly*

wouldn't be good enough. "If there are a few things not so shiny, what do we do to make them shiny?"

"I've got a guy for that too. I'll give you his number and you can meet. He'll clean up whatever needs to be cleaned up. Luke, I have your back."

Luke believed him. He'd known Dave since college. He'd even been one of the groomsmen at Dave's wedding nearly twenty years ago. Luke knew Dave would fight like hell to get his name cleared. The only question was: how long would it take?

CHAPTER TWENTY-FOUR

MARCUS

Marcus tapped the end of his yellow highlighter onto the stack of papers balancing on his lap. On the drive down to Bakersfield to interview Howard and Eleanor Davis, he'd reviewed the past year's worth of phone records for both Luke and Kendall. He couldn't find a single connection between the two, prior to May of that year, which is exactly when they both had claimed they reconnected. What was Marcus missing? He had found potentially interesting information, but nothing connecting Kendall and Luke. He set down the pen and said, "I don't know. I don't see any connection between Luke and Kendall prior to George's death."

"Buddy, I don't know how you can read in the car. I'd be barfing out the window by now. That's a serious skill you have."

Marcus crossed his arms and leaned back. "So, what do you think?"

"Maybe they used burner phones? Email? Although both Luke and Kendall seem far too intelligent to plot a murder by email. From what Luke's colleagues said, he's brilliant and not likely to keep a paper trail for plotting a murder. I hate to say it, but if Luke ordered a hit on George to reclaim his lost love, it may be really hard to prove it. Unless we can get Dratch to talk."

"Agree. We should be hearing from the district attorney's office soon about the deal." Marcus was beginning to believe, as did Gates, that the only way to crack this case was to get Dratch to talk, telling them what he knew. Currently, Dratch had absolutely no motivation to confess who had hired him. Marcus had put in a request with the DA to make a deal with Dratch to encourage him to cooperate. He set the papers down. "However, there is one repeat phone number, all incoming to Luke's cell phone. And they're mostly short, less than two minutes, almost daily for the last year. Odd."

"Any idea who it is?" Gates asked.

Marcus shook his head. "No idea."

"Give it a call and find out who answers?"

"On it."

Marcus pulled out his cell phone and dialed the number. A man's voice answered in a hushed tone. "Hello."

Marcus eyed Gates from across the front seat. "Hello, I found a cell phone and am trying to find the owner, may I ask who this is?"

Silence.

Marcus looked at the screen, and it flashed the message *call ended*.

"I'll say this much, it was someone who didn't want to talk to me or any other stranger." Marcus made a note to put in a request to find out who the number belonged to. Something was off about Luke Abbington, and he'd figure out what it was.

Gates slowed the sedan and said, "We're here."

Marcus studied the house of Eleanor and Howard Davis. It had a freshly mown lawn and well-maintained wood siding. From the corner of his eye, he saw the ruffle of curtains behind the front window. Whoever was inside was aware of their presence.

Marcus turned to Gates. "Time to see what we can find out from George's family."

"Hopefully something, because I'm feeling like we've got a whole lot of nothing. And after that drive, let's hope this was worth it."

Marcus didn't mind the four-hour drive down to Bakersfield, because it had given him the time to review the phone records and come up with a line of questioning for George's family. It was one avenue they hadn't explored since the case had escalated to murder, mostly due to the proximity of their residence.

Gates rapped on the front door. It opened within moments. In front of them stood Howard Davis, George's brother. He was tall, a bit pudgy, dark hair, and dark eyes. A bit shifty. Marcus wouldn't be surprised if he was an ex-addict or someone who hid their addiction from most of the world. Was it Howard who'd spotted them through the curtains?

Before either Marcus or Gates could speak, Howard said, "Detectives, what a surprise. I wish you would've called. Mother isn't doing well."

Gates stepped closer. "Unfortunately, in these matters, sometimes there's no time to call ahead. We'll only take a few minutes of your time."

Marcus didn't think it was lost on Howard that they had driven four hours and could've easily called to set up a time.

Gates continued, "May we come in? We have a few questions for you and your mother."

Howard stepped back. "Sure, please come in. My mother's in bed, so I'll have to let her know you're here. You can wait in the living room on the left."

The detectives stepped into the home. It was clean and tidy, with furnishings dating back to the 1980s, including a coral and teal color scheme. The faint scent of roses filled the air. Based on the state of the home, it appeared Howard took good care of his mother.

Howard returned. "Can I get you anything to drink?"

Both detectives declined a beverage and sat on the sofa. Howard took a seat across from them in a chair. "So, what can I help you with?"

"Is your mother not joining us?" Gates asked.

"Unfortunately, her health has taken a turn for the worse recently. She stays in bed these days. Liver cancer."

"I'm so sorry. Will she be up for a few questions?"

"Yes, but I thought we'd speak first."

"Great. As you know, we've arrested the man responsible for the car accident that killed your brother. What you may not know is that there's been a new development in the case, and we have reason to believe that Irwin Dratch, the driver of the vehicle, was hired to kill your brother. Your brother's death is now an open murder investigation."

Howard's face remained still and his body rigid. No signs of shock or interest. Marcus knew this could mean many things. Either Marcus was in shock and didn't have a reaction, or it could mean that he already knew. Perhaps Kendall had talked to him? Or he'd seen it on the news?

Howard crossed his legs. "That's awful. I can't imagine who would want to kill my brother. He was loved by everyone. A real golden boy. Handsome and athletic. He could have any girl he wanted, ever since we were kids."

Marcus wondered if there was a hint of resentment in Howard's voice. Marcus asked, "Can you think of anybody that may want to harm your brother? An old girlfriend from school? High school or college? Anyone with the slightest grudge."

Howard shook his head. "No. Everybody loved George. Everyone."

Gates maneuvered in his seat. "Sounds like George was a great guy. I believe that's pretty much what everybody's told us so far in the investigation. But being his brother and all, we were hoping you'd be able to share some insight the others couldn't."

"Not that I can think of. As I said, everybody loved the guy."

Marcus studied Howard, watching his legs uncross and then cross again, but the expression on his face was steady, his voice too. "How often did you talk to your brother before he passed?"

Howard shifted his arms, leaning over on one elbow. "About once a week. He always called to check on Mom. I usually answered the phone, and we'd do a quick catch up before I handed the phone to her."

Marcus prodded. "So, you two weren't particularly close?"

Howard's demeanor changed to one of defensiveness. "We didn't really have a lot in common other than our DNA. George was the studious go-getter. Sports. Honor roll, that sorta thing. School wasn't for me. I prefer to work with my hands."

Gates cocked his head. "And what do you do for work?"

"I haven't worked outside of taking care of Mom for the last couple of years. Before that, I did—you know, odd jobs—like construction and also worked in warehouses. It was good, honest work, but when Mom was diagnosed, I was only the one who would take care of her. George was too busy with his job and life in the Bay Area. So I did what I had to."

Maybe Marcus was wrong about Howard. Maybe he wasn't shifty. Maybe he was just tired. Being a caretaker of an elderly parent with cancer was no cakewalk. But on the other hand, maybe he was resentful toward his brother for not helping out more with the day-to-day, essentially leaving Howard with all the responsibility. Marcus added, "Sounds rough."

"It can be challenging. But we're family. You're supposed to take care of family."

Gates pushed himself off the sofa. "I hear you. Looks like you've been doing a great job. Do you think we can speak to your mother now?"

Howard stood. "Of course, please follow me, she's down the hall. I let her know you were here so that she could prepare herself. George's death has been hard on her. I'm not sure how she'll take the news that it wasn't an accident."

The detectives followed Howard down the hallway to the first bedroom on the right. Marcus entered first and gave a friendly smile to Eleanor Davis, who was propped up in a hospital bed.

She smiled, and her whole face crinkled. Gates approached her left side. "Mrs. Davis, my name is Detective Gates, and this is my partner, Detective Rogers. It's nice to meet you."

She gently placed her hands across her lap. "It's very nice to meet you two boys. Thank you so much for finding who hurt my boy."

Gates said, "That's actually why we're here, Mrs. Davis. We found the person who committed the crime, the one who was driving the car, but now we think he didn't act alone." He hesitated before telling her more. "It wasn't an accident. Somebody hired that man to kill your son."

The wide-eyed, glassy look on Mrs. Davis's face told everything. Shock, horror, and devastation all rolled into one.

Marcus thought back to Howard's reaction to the news; it was none of that. Howard had to have already known. He didn't think the news of the murder-for-hire plot would be broadcast as far south as Bakersfield, but he also hadn't checked. Marcus stepped to the right side of the bed. "Mrs. Davis, we're sorry to have to tell you this. I'm sure it's unsettling, but if you can think of anybody who might have wanted to hurt George, it would be helpful."

Howard rushed to her side, tissues in hand. "Mom, take your time. Take your time."

Mrs. Davis accepted the tissue from Howard and dabbed the tears at the corners of her eyes. "I'm fine. Honestly, I can't think of anyone. He was a wonderful son. A wonderful husband. Oh, how he loved Kendall. Such a sweet girl. I never had a chance to know her very well due to how far apart we lived, but every time I saw her, she was just a delight. I know how George felt for her, and she was good for him. I was grateful that he'd found someone to love him and someone for him to love. You really can't ask much more for your children than for them to be happy and to know a love like that. Such a lovely woman. She's called every month since George died, just to see how I'm doing."

Marcus nodded at Mrs. Davis. He wondered how much longer she had on this earth. Her skin was pale with a yellow tint, and her eyes were sunken in. "Mrs. Davis, can you think of anyone at all who would want to hurt your son?" he asked one more time, to be sure.

"No, I really can't. Why would anyone hurt my boy on purpose?" She glanced over at Howard. "Can you think of anyone?"

Howard leaned up against the wall next to her bed. "No, Mom. I really can't. Everyone loved George."

At the sound of the doorbell, they all turned their heads toward the entry of the room. "Expecting someone?" Gates asked.

Mrs. Davis said, "It must be the lawyer. He was supposed to come over to update my will. Apparently, it's a bit out of date."

How was it out of date? Hadn't she been sick for quite some

time? He assumed her affairs would've been in order. Perhaps it still named George as a beneficiary.

Howard left the room without a word.

Marcus said, "Well, ma'am, if you can think of anything that could help, please give us a call. I'll leave our card with Howard. Thank you very much for talking with us today."

They headed down the hall and turned into the living room, where Howard stood with a man in a gray suit and receding hairline. Something flickered inside Marcus.

Gates approached Howard. "Thank you for letting us come in and talk to you and your mother. We'll do everything we can to bring justice for George. Here's my card. Please call if you think of any information or if you have any questions."

Howard took the card and nodded.

Marcus approached the lawyer and extended his hand. "I'm Detective Rogers. I understand you're Mrs. Davis's lawyer?"

"Yes, Frank Miller, I'm here to update the will. Unfortunately, I hear from Howard that she only has a month or two left. If they're lucky."

Marcus cocked his head. "She didn't have her affairs in order prior?"

The lawyer nodded. "Yes, she did, but there's a bit of housekeeping to do. We need to remove George from the will, which will make it easier for Kendall when the time comes. The poor woman has been through enough."

"What do you mean 'easier for Kendall'?" Howard asked.

Both detectives focused their attention on Howard. Marcus observed Howard's body stiffen, visibly agitated.

The lawyer continued. "With the removal of George, she won't need to worry about it going through George's probate. It will go directly to her."

Howard's eyes widened. "Kendall is in the will?"

"Yes. Your mother wanted both of them to be named."

Obviously, it was the first Howard had heard that Kendall was listed in his mother's will. After Mrs. Davis's glowing review of Kendall during their interview, it wasn't terribly surprising, although a little unusual that she'd included her daughter-in-law.

Howard flicked his hand in the air. "Oh, of course. It must have slipped my mind."

Yeah, right. Marcus faced the lawyer. "It was nice to meet you. Do you have a card?"

The lawyer reached inside his jacket and pulled out a card. "If you ever have the need for estate planning, trusts, or wills, which everyone should have, give me a call anytime."

BACK ON THE HIGHWAY, MARCUS SAID, "WHAT DID YOU make of that? Last-minute update to remove George from the will? Any idea how much Mrs. Davis's estate is worth?"

"No, but you and I were thinking the same thing. Put in a request to pull her financials. It could be important. We may have a third person with a possible reason to want George out of the picture. Maybe resentment for having to take care of his mother on his own. Didn't think George deserved it? The only thing that makes me hesitate on Howard is that I doubt he has the means to hire a hitman. I doubt Dratch comes cheap. So how would he have come up with the money?"

Marcus said, "Maybe he has power of attorney over Mrs. Davis's bank accounts. He could have used his mother's money to put a hit on his brother."

"That's some dark shit."

Dark, yes, but it was also a solid motive. "I'll request the financial records for both Howard and Eleanor Davis. Hopefully, we'll get them ASAP." Marcus's adrenaline rushed through him. His gut was talking, and it was saying he was on the right track. Giddy about the new lead, his stomach suddenly soured. "Shit."

"Do tell."

"If Howard hired Dratch to inherit the entirety of his mother's estate, and he didn't know Kendall was named in the will . . ."

Gates finished his thought. "She could be a target. If he's our guy. Although I'm not yet convinced he is. I still like Luke for this."

Marcus realized they needed to get Irwin Dratch to talk—and fast.

CHAPTER TWENTY-FIVE

KENDALL

Kendall munched on her sesame bagel as she tried to focus on the performance of the S&P 500 on her laptop monitor. It was useless. It was becoming more and more difficult to think of anything other than the investigation and the suspicions that had fallen upon her and Luke. Kendall's concentration shifted at the sound of a knock on the door. She shut the laptop, set down her half-eaten bagel, and ambled over to let Selena in. She was right on time. They'd spoken the previous day on the phone, and Selena had assured Kendall that she and her team would get to the bottom of the case as soon as possible.

She peered through the peephole at a woman with dark hair up in a messy bun, presumably Selena. This morning's in-person meeting was to be their first debrief and overview of the plan for investigating George's murder. Kendall hoped the investigation would clear not only her name, but Luke's too. Even if she wasn't sure of their relationship, she knew she wasn't ready for him to walk out of her life.

She opened the door and did a double take. Based on their phone conversation, Kendall would've guessed Selena Bailey was six feet tall and an Olympic athlete. More in line with the looks of her lawyer, Cybil. Instead, before her stood a younger-looking woman, no more than five foot three inches tall, with a slight build. The all-black attire and multiple piercings on both ears made her seem more like a defiant teenager than a seasoned private investigator. Despite the Gothic appearance, Selena was beautiful—with clear, olive skin and brown Disney-princess eyes. *Talk about not judging a book by its cover.* "Hello, you must be Selena."

She extended her slender hand to Kendall. "Selena Bailey, private investigator at your service, Ms. Murphy."

Kendall shook her hand. "Please come inside, and call me Kendall."

They sat on the sofa, facing one another. Selena didn't waste any time. She pulled out her gray laptop from her black leather shoulder bag. "How are you holding up?"

Kendall shrugged. "I'm okay. Distracted. Can't wait for this to be over."

"I hear you. What are you doing to keep busy?"

She smirked. "I was trying to work, but . . . failing."

"Have you considered taking a leave of absence or taking some PTO until this is over?"

Kendall hadn't. It wasn't a bad idea. She'd make a mental note to discuss it with her boss. She didn't want to put her clients financial health at risk. A colleague, or three, should be able to take over her accounts temporarily. "No, but I will. Thanks."

"No prob. You okay if we jump right in?"

Kendall nodded.

"Since we spoke yesterday, I was able to start on the investigation. I thought we would first review some of the preliminary findings and then move on to the next steps." She flipped open the lid of her laptop. "The goal of our investigation is to formulate a plausible alternate theory for who hired Irwin Dratch to kill George. In order to do that, I reviewed all the current records provided by the police to your lawyer. Luckily, the detectives have been very cooperative, which they don't have to be at this stage, since you aren't an official suspect and haven't been charged." Selena glanced down at the screen and then at Kendall. "I'm assuming you already know this. What you may not realize is that Irwin Dratch is a seasoned hitman. My team put out some feelers, and word on the street is he's good—one of the best—and expensive. My guys say it's shocking he was caught. This is good news for two reasons. First, it means the detectives investigating the case are also very good. Second, this helps us know that whoever hired him had to have the means to do so. We're talking upwards of a hundred grand."

Kendall let that settle in. Who in her and George's life could afford that? *Luke.* Yes, he could afford it, but he wouldn't. Did she know that for sure? There were coworkers too. Neighbors. Who else? "Somebody wealthy did this?"

"Appears so. Or someone with access to a lot of cash."

Kendall wondered how Selena had come by this information. "How do you know this about Dratch?"

Selena kept a straight face. "I can't disclose my sources or methods. It's for your protection and mine. If I told you, I'd have to kill you."

Kendall's eyes widened and her mouth gaped.

Selena chuckled. "I'm sorry, that was a bad joke. I couldn't resist."

Kendall shook her head and smiled, embarrassed. "I need to be less gullible, I suppose." Was she gullible?

Selena shook her head. "No, no. You're just on edge."

Kendall shrugged. "I suppose."

"Um, before I move on to the next steps, I need to ask you something." She paused. "Have you talked to Luke?"

Kendall's smile faded. "Not since Saturday—two days ago."

Selena's expression softened. "Good."

Her heart pounded. "I know not to talk to him, but why do you seem so relieved? What aren't you telling me?"

"My team has initiated surveillance of select individuals. Luke is one of them."

Kendall froze, and Selena eyed her.

"I'm only telling you this so that you keep your distance and to keep you safe."

"Tell me what?"

"Luke met with an unknown male with whom he exchanged money. The person he met with did not appear to be a law-abiding citizen. And I'll just be frank with you: it looked like some kind of payoff. At this point, we don't have the name of the person he met with or understand the true nature of the exchange, but it doesn't make him look innocent. If he did kill your husband to be with you, you need to stay away from him."

Kendall processed the information. Luke paying someone off ... Was it possible he could have killed George? The Luke she knew or *thought* she knew, couldn't have. Could he? She shook the thoughts from her head. It was too much.

"I know this is hard to hear. It doesn't mean he's guilty, but my team has started putting together a scenario for an alternate theory.

"That's it?" What happened to "best in the business"? One look at Luke and it was over?

"Not by a long shot. It's just one potential scenario. I want to remind you that our main focus is to prove you're not guilty and to provide reasonable doubt. We have to find somebody who had motive to kill your husband. We're also looking into coworkers, former girlfriends, acquaintances, and associates."

"What are the 'next steps'?"

"Yes, next steps. We'll obtain video footage before and after George's death, not only of George, but of our entire list of interesting persons. We'll also look at the financials, and we'll do background checks as well."

"How long do you think your investigation will take?"

"The plan has already been set into motion. I have a team reviewing surveillance footage from the weeks prior to your husband's death, as well as after."

Kendall interrupted. "You have video of George? From where?"

"At and around work, home, the gym, and other places. We're using traffic and street cameras. If somebody was blackmailing him or meeting with him secretly or being seen in any kind of altercation, we'll hopefully see it and be able to piece together a motive."

"Have you found anything out of the ordinary?" Had George been hiding something from her?

"Not yet."

Kendall sank back into the sofa, contemplating what Selena had told her. "What can I do to help?"

Selena cocked her head. "Help?"

"I want to help with the investigation. There must be something I can do," Kendall pleaded.

Selena studied the screen on her laptop. Without looking up she said, "Maybe. First, I have to give you a disclaimer. I should've explained. Everything I've shared with you today can't be shared with anybody, especially not the police. I told you we have special methods, and special doesn't always mean legal. That said, I don't want to put you in a position where you could be culpable. Some methods we use are less quote-unquote special than others. I think maybe you could help with those items. Give me some time to put together a plan for you, okay?"

"Thank you. I need to do something."

"I hear you." Selena looked around. "I'd go nuts if I were

locked in a room all day. Wait," she said, "I almost forgot the good news. We cleared Beth to visit you."

Knowing her best friend could visit took some weight off her shoulders. "I'll call her." Then she hesitated. "What about Luke?"

"What about Luke?" Selena asked.

Kendall explained. "I'm not supposed to talk to him, but should I call him to confront him? I could find out who he was meeting with." She had to know.

"Between you and me, I don't think I could wait either. If you trust him, really trust him—now don't tell Cybil I said this—you could ask him about it." She raised up her hands. "I mean on the phone. Not in person. Absolutely not in person."

Would she do it? *Could* she do it?

"I need to go, but I'll call you soon with your plan and any other updates we may have for you, okay?"

Kendall nodded.

"Call Beth. Have a night off from all of this."

"Will do." Beth always had a way of cheering her up and making her laugh even in the darkest times. And after she called Luke, she might need a heck of a lot of cheering up.

Kendall remained on the sofa and waved as Selena left her hotel room. She thought about her next move - confronting Luke, on the phone, not in person. She had to hear his side of the story. What had he been doing in that exchange? What was he hiding? She picked up her phone and stared at Luke's information.

Her nerves rattled as she contemplated the conversation ahead. What if he confessed to killing George? She would be responsible for his death. How could she live with herself? An hour ago, she wouldn't have even questioned if Luke could have had anything to do with George's death. She'd really like some good news at some point.

It was now or never.

She pressed call.

He answered after one ring.

"Kendall! I'm so happy to hear from you."

The sound of his voice made her heart ache. It'd been two days since they last spoke. It was the longest they had gone without talking since the day of Janine's graduation. "Me too."

"Is it over, did your team find out who killed George?"

"Um, no. I . . . need to ask you about something."

"What is it?"

Woman up, Kendall. "Don't ask me how I know this, but I was told something, and I need you to tell me the truth. Did you meet with someone? Someone that you paid off, or at least it appeared that way. I need you to explain to me what they saw."

The silence from the other end of the phone was stifling.

Why wasn't he answering?

A sinking feeling descended over her.

"It's not what you think. I swear to you I had nothing to do with George's death."

"What was it about? I need to hear it from you. I need 100 percent honesty if we're to continue this relationship." She exhaled the breath she didn't know she was holding. What secret dealings did Luke have with shady characters? And why hadn't he told her before? Was nothing as it seemed?

"I don't want to do this over the phone. I need you to trust me. I'll tell you what was going on. Can I see you?"

"I'm not supposed to be seen with you, Luke. If the press finds out that you're visiting me or where my location is, that'll be bad, really bad."

Not to mention if he had killed George, would he kill her, too, to cover it up? She couldn't believe she was having these thoughts about her *boyfriend*.

"Please let me meet you. I'll explain everything. Kendall,

I'm telling you, I had absolutely nothing to do with his death. I didn't hire someone to kill him. I didn't want him to be harmed. I would never put you through that kind of pain. I know you loved him."

The comment about her love for George caught her off guard like a punch to the gut. Was Luke sincere? If he wasn't involved in George's death, what was he involved in? Could she trust Luke?

CHAPTER TWENTY-SIX

KENDALL

Kendall spit out her wine as she laughed at Beth's latest story about a Tinder meetup that had gone terribly wrong. Beth said, "Count yourself as one of the lucky ones, not having to be subjected to online dating. It's the worst."

"I don't know. Maybe I'll need it sooner than I think."

"What about Luke?"

Kendall still hadn't decided what to do about Luke. Selena had given her damning evidence that something was not right with him. He'd sworn he had nothing to do with George's death and insisted he would explain everything in person. She needed time to process it all, and she was relieved Beth was free to spend the evening with her, drinking and eating pepperoni pizza. It was exactly what she needed.

"We'll see if we survive this investigation."

Both their eyes flicked down to the coffee table as Kendall's cell phone buzzed. Beth said, "Speak of the devil. Are you gonna answer it?"

Kendall shook her head. "No." She hadn't agreed to see him and didn't want him trying to persuade her.

"No? Are you still not supposed to talk to him?"

"Not really, but we did talk. There's some weird stuff going on, but I don't really want to talk about it."

Beth slumped in her comfy couch seat. "I'm sorry to hear that. Well, at least I brought a second bottle of wine!" Beth smiled.

Kendall glanced down at the empty bottle of Pinot on the table. "Did we drink that entire bottle?" No wonder Kendall was feeling more at ease. She was about a glass away from drunk. She couldn't wait.

Beth pulled the other bottle out of her shopping bag.

Kendall said, "You're the perfect friend."

"Yes, yes, I am. So, have you been able to talk to Janine and Grandma?"

"Janine is staying with a friend because they're afraid the press will go after her as well. But she'll be moving into a new place pretty soon."

The lack of noise from the television was nice. Kendall had decided to leave the TV off for a while, and she hoped that the "killer couple" would be old news soon so she could leave the hotel room and maybe even salvage her reputation.

She was torn about Luke. What could he be doing that was so shady he was meeting suspicious fellows and giving them money? What didn't she know about him? A lot.

Kendall's phone buzzed on the coffee table once again. Beth said, "Wow. Aren't you miss popularity?"

Kendall snatched the phone from the table. "Hello."

"Hi, Kendall," Selena said. "I received some news, and I thought you'd want to know right away."

Kendall set down her glass of wine. "What is it?"

"We're working on the background check for the person who met with Luke in the park. We don't have anything definitive yet, but it's looking like it has nothing to do with

George's death. I still need to confirm this, so it's not a fact yet, but it's leaning that way."

Relief fell over her like a cool blanket. She really wanted to believe the best about Luke. "I couldn't wait a day, so I already called him. After you told me about what you found, I wanted to hear from him what it was about. He swears it had nothing to do with George's death, but he wanted to explain everything to me in person. But—"

Selena's voice was stern. "Don't let him come over yet. Give me a day."

"I haven't given him an answer."

"I may be erring on the side of caution here, but I wouldn't be able to live with myself if I put you in harm's way. My team is the best there is, and they will find out if Luke is a safety risk or not. But, to be honest, more women should run background checks on a prospective partner. You just happen to have a more urgent need. Look at it this way, if Luke is who he says he is, I'll be able to verify it. And then you'll never have to worry again. It's much better to know now, than to find out a year or five years from now, when it could be too late. So, please, just wait."

Kendall wondered how Selena had wisdom beyond her years. The woman couldn't be more than twenty-five. Yet Kendall could hear the caution in Selena's voice. Selena really didn't want her to meet with Luke.

"Okay, I'll wait. Thank you, Selena. I do appreciate everything you and your team are doing."

"I'll be in touch. Take care."

Kendall set her phone back down on the coffee table. Beth was staring at her and tapping her fingers on the glass in her hands, waiting impatiently for the update. "What was that about?"

Kendall explained the whole kit and caboodle. So much for not talking about it. Wine must be the liquid truth serum.

Beth said, "Wow. She makes an excellent point. All of us out there using dating apps and websites, how do we know that anybody is who they say they are? I mean, do you ever really know anyone?"

"All women need a Selena in their life! I'm telling you, she is a total badass. She has a whole team of investigators, and they've got to be black ops or something. She finds bad guys and saves people's lives. Well, assuming she saves mine. I have faith she will. Jeez. All I do is work on investment accounts and study the stock market. I'm super lame."

"No, you're not. You're a badass at what you do. Who knows the stock market better than you? It's pretty cool the way you look at numbers all day." Beth held a blank expression, and then she smiled.

They both fell into a fit of laughter.

Kendall screeched, "My job is boring."

Beth fell to the side of the couch and laughed harder.

Kendall joined her. "Maybe it's time I do something different."

Beth pulled off her glasses and wiped the corners of her eyes with the edge of her shirt. "You're only thirty-five, you could do a career change if you really wanted to." She added, "You're not dead yet!"

After they finished their giggle-fest, Kendall thought over the idea. After all she'd been through the last year, it made her wonder if she was in the right profession or doing enough with her life. Her entire job consisted of making more money for people who already had enough money. What impact was she making on the world? Maybe she couldn't focus on work because she realized it just wasn't that important.

"No, no. You're right. I should change careers."

"You're getting way too serious for my buzz. Yeah, maybe

your job is a little boring and a little like it's all about money and the man and whatever, but what would you rather do?"

"I don't know. What should I do with my life? Something to better mankind."

Beth chortled. "Okay, now we've reached into the drunken-philosopher stage of this visit. Time to switch course. I want to hear more about Luke. Have you guys—you know?"

Kendall couldn't stop the smile that crept across her face.

Beth said, "That good?"

Kendall said, "Well, he is pretty fucking hot. Oh man, Beth. He is so . . . I almost don't care if he's a criminal. No, I do care. I do. I don't want him to be a criminal. But gosh, Beth, he fills me up in every way. When I'm with him, I feel like I'm on cloud nine, and the rest of the world melts away. So. Lame. I know."

"Oh no girl, you're just in love."

Yeah, I'm in love with a murder suspect. She hoped he wasn't guilty. Really, really hoped. In her heart, she didn't think he was capable of such a heinous act.

Beth picked up her phone, and her mouth dropped open. "Oh, dang. Facebook is blowing up."

Oh God not about me, right? "Why, what is it?" Kendall asked.

"There was a shooting at a nightclub here in San Francisco. Oh my God." Beth continued to scroll her phone. "We should turn on the news."

Kendall hesitated before stumbling over to her nightstand to reach the remote. She flicked on the news. It was awful. Sirens and cell phone videos of gunshots. *Why do people keep doing this?* The carnage made her sick to her stomach.

Kendall yelled at the television, "Why can't we all just fucking get along? You do you. I do me. Let's all just let each other *be* already!"

Beth nodded. "Yeah, what is with these motherfuckers?"

Then another thought popped in Kendall's head. "Oh, Beth. I am rotten. To the core." Kendall shook her head. She was a bad person. *So bad*.

Beth looked over her shoulder at her. "What? Why?"

Kendall grimaced. "Because I thought . . . maybe this means I'm no longer front-page news."

"It doesn't mean you wanted this."

"Of course not!"

Kendall nodded as she thought about what this meant. Could she go outside of her hotel-slash-prison-room? Could she see Luke? No, no, she'd wait for Selena. She should wait for Selena, right?

CHAPTER TWENTY-SEVEN

MARCUS

Detective Rogers and Detective Gates sat across from Irwin and his expensive lawyer. Each pair stared at the other as if to size the other one up. Dratch spoke crisply, "I'm assuming we're not here for brunch, so why don't you get on with it."

His lawyer twirled the corner of his mustache and said, "I agree, my client would prefer his cell than to talk to the two of you, so if you have something you want to say, let's hear it."

Marcus knew Dratch was slick. When he first met him, he assumed he was a bit of a bumbling fool. He was tall and thick, reminding him of a retired basketball player or a friend's weird uncle. But now Marcus knew better. "Well, Mr. Dratch, as you may or may not be aware, we've connected you to several homicides in the state. The charges are piling up."

Gates grinned. "The Golden State doesn't take kindly to murderers."

Dratch's lawyer cocked his head toward Gates. "Are we here for you to harass my client or is there something you'd like to share with us—something we don't already know?"

Gates tipped his head at Marcus.

Marcus said, "We would like to make a deal with you, Mr. Dratch. In exchange for information and subsequent testimony leading to the arrest of the person who hired you to kill George Davis, the DA is willing to drop the charge from capital murder to second-degree murder. You take the deal, and maybe you'll get out of jail before you die. Or you can take your chances that the moratorium on the death penalty in the state of California remains in place."

Marcus doubted that the moratorium made by the governor of California in 2019, suspending all executions in California, would be undone anytime soon. But it was worth mentioning in order to pressure Dratch.

Gates shrugged. "I don't know, if it were me, I'd be concerned the governor's term is only four years and that maybe the next governor will feel differently about capital punishment. A new governor is sworn in and the next thing you know—bam." Gates slammed his hands on the table. "You've got a needle in your arm."

Irwin Dratch placed his thick hands on the table and eased down in his chair, squinting his cold eyes to stare directly into Marcus's. An evil grin hopped up on one side of his face. "You still haven't figured it out yet. Did I not make it easy enough for you? Don't tell me this is your first murder investigation? Well, it sounds like the only way you're going to catch this person you seek is if I tell you. Am I right about that?"

The detectives exchanged glances.

Marcus hated that Dratch knew he was a rookie and that he seemed completely unaffected by their entire exchange.

Marcus feigned indifference. "We have inquiries into multiple suspects, and new leads come in each day. But yes, it would make our investigation go a little quicker if we could get you to cooperate. Consider it your lucky day."

Dratch leaned back in his chair and folded his arms across his chest. "Bullshit. You've got nothing."

Dratch's lawyer interrupted. "Why don't you give my client and me a few minutes to discuss your offer. Alone."

Marcus said, "Sure." He turned to Gates. "Let's leave these two gentlemen to discuss our offer."

"Of course." Gates met Dratch's gaze. "Just give the door a tap when you're ready for us." He tipped his chin and sauntered out of the interrogation room.

Outside the room, they waited. "What did you think of that?" Marcus had a bad feeling. Dratch was too cocky and too relaxed for someone who should've been afraid of spending the rest of his life in prison.

"I think he'll counter with something more. The guys down in LA say they think he has mob connections. This guy is smart, a lot smarter than we gave him credit for. And I'm pretty sure his lawyer's suit cost more than my car. There's no way he'll take the deal. This is likely an act. They already have a plan devised for what they want in return for his testimony."

Marcus contemplated it. If Dratch and his lawyer were as clever as they thought, chances were they'd been waiting until the investigation started lagging to give their demands. It made him sick.

A rap on the door from inside the interrogation room drew Marcus from his thoughts.

Marcus and Gates returned to their original seats and waited.

Dratch's lawyer spoke first. "My client is willing to give you full disclosure of what he knows about the person who paid him to kill George Davis, which he'll disclose once a deal is in place. Here is what we want in return. First, I'd like my client moved to a private cell immediately. He's currently being housed with disgusting, filthy criminals. Second, my client will serve his time in a minimum-security prison, since, as you know, he poses no threat to society. He's never wished anyone harm, nor does he now. He was simply a worker bee in the grander scheme of things. In return, my client will admit to his part in the crime, plead guilty to vehicular manslaughter, hit-and-run, and grand theft auto."

Before Marcus responded, Dratch's lawyer added, "And we want it all in writing. My client won't say another word until a deal is penned and signed by the district attorney."

Marcus deflated. Was he serious? Or was this a stalling tactic?

Gates said, "We'll take your terms to the DA. You'll hear from us."

They stood up and the detectives left the interrogation room. Strutting back to the office, Marcus asked, "Will the DA go for that? Minimum security for a known hitman, with multiple murders?"

"The DA might in order to prosecute the person who gave the order to kill George Davis. It's a high-profile case, and the state will want the win. Dratch is old, and he didn't kill for fun —that we know of. I don't know, buddy. All we can do is try. I honestly don't think he'll take less than everything he has asked for."

As much as Marcus wanted the case closed, it didn't seem right for a career hitman to receive minimum-security prison on reduced charges. What price was too high to catch one bad guy? On the other hand, the idea of putting the case behind him was enticing. The case had been eating away at him. His days and nights were filled with nothing but the investigation. His partner had been right. If Marcus didn't find a better way to cope with the job, he was done for.

CHAPTER TWENTY-EIGHT

KENDALL

From underneath the comforter, Kendall pulled her phone off the nightstand and slid it up to her ear. She grumbled, "Hello."

"I'm sorry, did I wake you? It's almost ten."

Ten o'clock? Thank God she'd talked to her boss and was officially on a leave of absence. To her surprise, her boss had been thrilled she'd brought it up. He said the publicity wasn't great for the firm. She'd thought, *Thanks for the support, asshole.*

How much wine had she and Beth drunk last night? She looked over at the other queen bed and saw Beth's electric-blue hair spilled across the pillow and her face covered by the comforter. Kendall guessed they'd drunk a lot. She vaguely remembered there being two bottles. She said to Selena, "Yeah, I'm fine. It's okay. Had a late night, inside."

"I wanted to call you right away with some news about Luke."

Kendall pushed back the covers and sat up. Her heart raced. "What is it?"

"My team looked into the person Luke met with. I don't want to explain everything yet, because I can tell how much you care for Luke. It's obvious. You mentioned that he wanted to come clean with you and set things straight. I'll let you talk to him and ask him about it. He'll likely have more details than my team can come up with. But the good news is, or at least the better news is, that it doesn't appear he's in any way connected to George's death. We haven't concluded our investigation, but I think it's unlikely he had anything to do with it. But I do think you should talk to him. I personally would want total honesty in a relationship. And this is something that's kind of big."

Kendall cleared her throat. Though happy about the news, she was also worried at the same time. What was this big thing that he needed to tell her? "Does that mean that I shouldn't be worried about my safety when I'm with Luke? Is it safe to talk to him or see him?" Her heart pounded. She hoped Selena had a good answer.

"Our investigation isn't done, but he seems like an okay guy. If you'd like, I could run a full background on him for your own personal information. Like I mentioned before, I truly believe all women should have a background done for a potential partner, especially someone like yourself who is worth quite a bit now. It's nothing to be ashamed of. You have to protect yourself. A lot of women are targets of men who are only after their money. And with the huge increase in online dating, someone online could be anyone. Sure, most are nice people looking for love, but in some cases, not so much. Have you heard about 'Dirty John'? He tried to kill his new wife's daughter! Terrible. If she had done a background check in the beginning, she might have avoided the whole messy situation. I met the wife at a convention, and she's giving the same advice now. It's better to be safe than sorry. *Trust me*."

Should she? Was that weird? Shouldn't she just trust him? "Is it terrible if I said yes?"

"Not at all."

"Can I ask, when you date somebody, do you do a background check on them?"

Selena laughed. "I don't date. But, if I did, I would. It's nothing to feel guilty about."

She was sure Luke had plenty of money, but it was better to be than safe than sorry, right? She was sure he'd come back clean. *Trust but verify.* "Okay. Do it."

"You got it."

Kendall chewed her lower lip. "Do you think it's okay to see him in person?"

"Well, the news has definitely shifted to more recent events. You're no longer the hot story, but things can change at any moment. The press could be back on you in the blink of an eye. It's probably okay if you want to have him come to the hotel so you can talk things through, but I'd recommend you don't be seen together in public, not until the case has been resolved."

Kendall relaxed. "Okay, I'll ask him to come over and to be discreet. Thank you, Selena. So, what about me? Can I go outside? Can I go on a walk outside of this hotel room?"

"I think if you wear the wig, hat, and glasses, you'll be okay. But not out with Luke."

"Noted."

Selena promised to be in touch. Part of her was thrilled at the possibility of seeing Luke sooner rather than later, but she was also uneasy about what he may tell her. Whatever it was, was serious enough that Selena didn't want to say. What could it be?

Later that day, butterflies fluttered in Kendall's stomach. She couldn't wait to see Luke. She opened the door to her hotel room and immediately wrapped her arms around his shoulders and pulled him into the hotel room, giving him a warm bearhug. Her doubts about him disappeared the moment his arms wrapped around her. He whispered in her ear, "I'm happy to see you too."

He took her hand and walked her over to the sofa and sat her down. "So, this is where you've been hiding out?" he said, looking around.

"This is it." She leaned in for another kiss.

After a moment passed, he gently pushed her back. "My God, I missed you, Kendall. There are so many things I absolutely want to do to you right now, but I think we should have a talk first."

Kendall's stomach dropped. *We should talk.* Never what you want to hear when you're in a relationship, even when you know it's coming.

"I want to explain." He stood and began pacing in front of the coffee table, running a hand through his hair.

"You can tell me, Luke. I'm sure it's not as bad as you think." *I hope.*

He stopped pacing and faced her. "Yes, I met somebody in the park and gave them money. But the truth is . . . I'm being blackmailed by Grace's cousin. A lowlife jerk. I never liked him, and he was never concerned about Grace when she was alive. Not even after she was diagnosed. But after her death, he was hellbent on getting part of her estate. He devised the idea that I somehow had a hand in Grace's death."

Kendall's mouth went dry. "But I thought she had cancer?"

Luke remained solemn. "She did. And toward the end, things were bad. She was in a lot of pain and on a lot of pain medication to ease her suffering. The thing is, and I don't know how her cousin knew this or maybe suspected it, but she asked me to give her too much. She wanted to go out of this world on her terms. I felt I owed that to her. I didn't administer anything.

But I did give her the medication and let her decide what was best for her. So, in some ways, I was complicit, but it's what she wanted. I assume he suspected something because the doctors had convinced the family that she had a few more months left, but then she died suddenly. He doesn't have any evidence or any proof that she overdosed herself, or that I gave it to her, but with everything going on, I just thought maybe I could make him go away."

"How long has he been blackmailing you?"

"It started six months after Grace's death. It began with a phone call, demanding money, saying that he knew what I'd done. He insisted Grace would've wanted him to have part of her estate. Really, he's just a degenerate looking for money and didn't care where he got it from or who he had to hurt to get it. I mostly ignored him and never planned to pay him off, but I certainly didn't want an air of suspicion right now. So, I met with him, paid him a large sum of money in cash, hoping it would keep him quiet."

Kendall's heart was heavy for him. After the agonizing death of his wife, he had to deal with a blackmailer. She pushed off the couch and rushed over to him, placing her on hand on his shoulder. "I'm so sorry you had to go through this, Luke. Please know I'm here for you."

He brushed her hair out of her face. "Thank you. I don't know what I would do without you. You've already made my world whole again." He leaned in for a sweet, soft kiss and then sat back. "So that's the story. Is there anything else you want to know?"

"Is there anything else I *should* know? Any illegitimate children or shady business deals or deals with the mob or, I don't know, parking tickets?"

He smiled. "I don't believe I have any parking tickets or mob ties or children, or what was the other?"

"Shady business deals." She grinned.

"None of those either." He placed his hands on her waistline and gazed into her eyes. "In some ways, I'm glad this came out. I want a future with you, and I don't want any secrets between us."

"Me too."

Luke kissed her softly, but Kendall couldn't hold back. She wrapped her arms around his neck and pushed him back onto the sofa. She climbed on top of him, hungry. He pulled back and asked, "Oh, are we doing this now?"

She nibbled on his earlobe and asked, "Why, is there something else you'd rather do?"

"Um, no, absolutely not—but there is one other small matter."

She leaned back, slightly hesitant. "What?"

"There is the whole we're murder suspects thing."

The fire inside of her extinguished. "Right." She untangled herself from Luke and sat next to him. "What are you thinking?"

He said, "What if we joined forces and fight to clear our names together instead of apart?"

"Do you think the lawyers will go for it?"

"First of all, the lawyers work for us, not the other way around. If we were arrested and went to trial, we would and should have separate counsel, but that's not what I'm suggesting. I propose we work together to figure out the truth. Once we find it, we can share it with the police to clear our names and get justice for George."

"I'll call Selena, my lead PI, and see what she thinks. I have to warn you though, she seems pretty capable of solving this alone and may not need or want outside help. She has a whole team."

"It's worth a try. More minds are better than fewer minds.

Maybe there's something both teams are missing. If we pull the two together to discuss what they've found, it could be exactly what we need."

Kendall studied Luke's face. He was handsome and brilliant. "It's a good idea. I'll call Selena now."

"Now?"

"I'm pretty sure she doesn't stop working, like ever."

Kendall's heart thudded in her chest as she dialed Selena. It was a great idea, and she hoped Selena thought so too. "Hi, Selena? I'm here with Luke, and we talked about everything."

"I'm glad to hear it."

"Anyway, that's not why I'm calling. Luke had an idea for us to join our teams to see if we can find the missing pieces, like in a brainstorming session. I'd like to be there too. Maybe I can help."

Kendall eyed Luke as she waited for a response from Selena.

Selena said, "Are you sure you want to do this? He hasn't been officially cleared by my team."

Kendall stared into Luke's brown eyes. "He's been cleared by me. And yes, I'm sure."

"It's not a bad idea. Let me discuss the details with my team. We can use a conference room at the hotel. Give Luke's team my information, we'll coordinate a time."

She beamed at Luke. "Great!"

"Kendall, take care and we'll talk soon."

She hung up the phone. "I have a good feeling about this, Luke."

"I do too." Luke pushed off the couch and extended his hand, and Kendall placed hers in his.

She followed his lead and walked over to the bed. Kendall stood at the edge and pulled her T-shirt over her head and threw it on the floor. Luke copied her, removing his black polo shirt.

Kendall bit her bottom lip, unhooked her black-lace bra, slipped off the straps, and tossed it on the floor.

Luke grabbed her by the waist and brought his lips to hers, inserting his tongue deep and forcefully. She moaned as electricity shot down her body. He slid off her blue jeans and gently pushed her back on the bed. He removed his black trousers and climbed on top of her. He kissed her forehead and then her nose. He paused at her lips. "Is it okay with you if I take my time, so that I can kiss every inch of your body?"

She shook her head and grinned. "No."

Luke's eyes widened. "No?"

She leaned forward and kissed him. "Tonight I'm not waiting. I want you now. Right now."

He kissed her deeply and then whispered, "As you wish."

Kendall let out a gasp as Luke fulfilled his promise.

CHAPTER TWENTY-NINE

KENDALL

Kendall bent over to kiss Luke, who was sitting on the sofa reading on his laptop. She tugged her cap lower to cover more of her face and said, "I'll be back in thirty minutes."

"Would you like me to order you breakfast while you're out?"

"Yes, please." She leaned over for another kiss.

"What do you want?"

"Eggs, toast, fruit, maybe sausage. Surprise me."

"You got it. Enjoy your walk."

The investigative teams had met twice over the last week. Selena assured her they were on the right track. It was a track that didn't include Luke or Kendall being guilty of murder.

She scurried over to the door. "Oh, I will. It's so nice to be able to leave this room. It's amazing what a little fresh air can do —so much better than being cooped up in a hotel room all day— even if it's a hotel room with you in it." She winked and waved, exiting the room.

Being sequestered in the hotel was a lot better when Luke was there. He'd come over on Wednesday and hadn't left. Five nights and mornings of Luke. She could definitely get used to waking up in his arms each day.

She stepped out the doors of the lobby, into the chilly air that smelled of garbage and car exhaust. She hurried down the street to reach the waterfront before the smell of dirty streets ruined her buzz. Her daily walks had invigorated her and brought her a newfound optimism. Things were finally starting to turn around. She knew better than to get her hopes up too high, after seeing how life can take a nosedive in the blink of an eye, but she had reasons to be optimistic that the investigation would be coming to a close pretty soon. The teams had been so busy she hadn't heard from Selena in several days.

She pressed the walk sign button on the stoplight and stared out across the bay. Even with San Francisco's fog, she could see the blue sky peeking out. She hurried across the street, heading straight for the trail.

Walking along the water, she felt more at peace than she had been in a long while.

Her lawyer and Selena kept assuring her this would all be over soon. She really hoped that it was true. She couldn't wait to start a new life in a new house. Not that she had found one yet, but she would. She'd even started contemplating a new job. After watching Selena and her team, she knew she needed to be doing something more meaningful with her life. Doing what exactly, she wasn't sure yet.

Maybe she could work in the nonprofit sector for an organization like the Innocence Project. Beth had turned her on to multiple documentaries and stories of those wrongly accused and victims of bad investigations by dirty cops. Kendall had had plenty of time during the last week to catch up on the shows. The wrongly convicted all had one thing in common—they couldn't afford a strong legal defense team.

Now having been falsely accused of a crime, she had a better understanding of how awful it could be.

She was fairly certain that Detective Rogers was not a dirty cop and he would do everything he could in his power to find the real truth. But you never know. She was feeling fortunate despite the turmoil of the last year. The music from her earbuds halted by an incoming call. She sighed. She hated when that happened. "Hello," Kendall answered.

"It's Selena. We have a solid theory and want to share it with the police right away. Can you meet us at the Ridgemont Police Station at eleven?"

"What is it—the theory, I mean?" She was curious, not having talked to Selena in a few days.

"I'd rather not discuss it over the phone. My team has prepared a presentation to hand over to the police. Can you meet us down at the station?"

"Yes, of course. I'll finish my walk and then head back to the hotel."

"Kendall, I recommend you cut your walk short and head back to the hotel now. Are you wearing your disguise?"

Her pulse quickened. "Why?"

"Please head back to the hotel, *now*." Selena replied, not answering her question.

"Okay." Relaxed vibes decimated, Kendall turned around and started on the trek back. "Do the detectives know we're coming?"

"Yes, Cybil just talked with Detective Rogers, and he's expecting us. I'm assuming Luke is with you. Let him know he's welcome to join us, but if he does, it's still better you take separate cars."

Kendall frowned. She had to remind herself that all of this was almost over, and her not being able to be seen in public with

Luke would be coming to an end, hopefully soon. She said, "Got it."

"Eleven o'clock at the Ridgemont Police Station."

After hanging up, Kendall was thrilled at the news of a working theory, but not thrilled that Selena hadn't answered her question. Was she in danger? Selena's lack of a response sounded like a yes.

She crossed a busy street and picked up her pace. A block further, she heard a voice call "Kendall" from behind her. She stopped and turned, peering down a side street. Her eyes went wide and her body froze.

CHAPTER THIRTY

MARCUS

Marcus nearly dropped his coffee at the sight of Kendall's lawyer and the woman standing next to her. Was she the lead PI, Selena Bailey? She was young and striking.

Marcus stood and approached Cybil and the attractive woman. "Cybil, nice to see you again, and you must be Selena."

Selena extended her hand. "Yes, I'm the lead PI in charge of the team working to clear Kendall's name and find out who killed George." She squeezed his hand, hard.

Ouch. *She bites.* Marcus wasn't sure what to make of her overconfident demeanor. He was charged with solving the murder of George Davis, not her, not some civilian. Was Selena trying to exude an air of dominance and power? She was petite, and quite frankly, stunning. Long wavy brown hair, flawless skin, and slightly curvy in the best way. He assumed the piercings were an attempt to conceal her beauty, but it failed miserably.

He loosened his grip. "Nice to meet you. I'm Detective Rogers. My partner will join us in a bit."

"Any sign of Kendall?" Selena asked.

Right to business. "Not yet."

Selena said, "Let's wait until Kendall arrives to go over the information. Like I mentioned to you on the phone, my team has drafted a few theories based on evidence that shows that both Kendall and Luke are not guilty of this crime. We do have a new suspect and want to share the information we have and hopefully help solve the case. But I really would like Kendall to be here."

"No problem. We can wait a bit. Can I get you any coffee? It's terrible, but it's coffee." He gave a lopsided grin.

Selena shook her head. "No, I'm properly caffeinated. Thank you. However, I do have slides I'd like to use for the presentation. Do you have a projector in the conference room where I can start setting up my equipment?"

Wow, she is all business. It was hot. He reminded himself to focus on the case and not Selena. Before he could give her directions, Gates called out from behind. "Selena?"

Marcus turned and studied his partner. His typically hard exterior had softened, and his usual stoic expression bore a surprised smile.

Selena grinned from ear to ear. "Detective Gates!"

They stepped closer to one another. Gates beamed at Selena. "How are you? I heard you were a PI now, one of the best, no surprise there. Wow. It's so great to see you."

How on earth did Gates know Selena? A former flame? Selena seemed far too young for him.

Selena's hard-ass persona had faded when she'd seen Gates. "I'm doing really well. It's good to see you too. I've meant to look you up over the years, but it's been hectic, especially since I took over for Martina." Sadness fell over Selena's face. "How are you? When did you transfer to Ridgemont?"

"Not long after." He paused. "About nine years ago."

She nodded.

Marcus interjected, "Selena was saying she needed a place to set up her slides."

"Let me show you," Gates offered.

Marcus said, "We'll wait out here for Kendall."

Marcus watched as they descended down the hallway to the conference room. He couldn't help but admire the swing of Selena's hips. He told himself to refocus, there was no time for that. And how the hell did Gates know her?

He turned to Cybil. "Have you heard the working theories? Does it seem rational, and more importantly, will it hold up in court?"

"The evidence isn't likely to hold up in court, but it could be obtained in a more legal-friendly manner, if needed."

Marcus hoped it was true. He'd never thought that Kendall could have done this, and he was confident his gut was correct. Kendall had been devastated at the death of her husband. The look in her eyes as she stood over his body was something that was burned into the back of his brain. He wondered if he'd ever be able to get the image out. He said, "I hope you're right. I'm looking forward to hearing the theory. We've also been waiting on a deal with the DA to get Dratch to talk."

"Boy, wouldn't that be nice and put an end to all of this. Where is Kendall? It's not like her to be late." Cybil stared down at her phone screen. "Maybe I'll try her again."

Marcus watched as Cybil placed the phone to her ear. She shook her head, indicating there was no answer. Something niggled in his gut. Kendall always answered her phone, unless there was a good reason not to. Maybe she was tied up with Luke? Maybe she was in a tunnel and couldn't get reception?

Fifteen minutes went by before Selena and Gates reentered the office area. "Still no Kendall? How about Luke? Have you tried calling him?" Selena asked.

Cybil said, "No, I haven't tried. I didn't know Luke would be joining us."

"I told her she could invite him, considering we'll be clearing his name too. However, he's not here either. That's odd."

Marcus turned to Selena. "Were they together?"

"When I spoke with Kendall earlier, she said Luke had been staying at the hotel with her. She was out for a walk when we spoke. I suggested they take separate cars to get here, so they're probably not together right now. Or . . ." Selena frowned.

Marcus's heart pounded. *Or she's in trouble.*

Selena continued, "Try Luke first before we begin to worry."

Marcus was growing more and more suspicious of the lack of either Luke or Kendall. Marcus didn't hesitate. He walked over to his desk to find Luke's phone number and tapped into his phone.

Luke answered after a single ring. "Hello?"

"Hi, Luke, this is Detective Rogers. Are you with Kendall? She was supposed to meet us."

"No, she's not with me. Why? Was she meeting you down there? Has something happened?"

"You don't know where Kendall is?" He glanced over at Selena.

Luke said, "No, she went out for a walk and then she texted me saying that she ran into a friend and was going to have breakfast with them at a café. But I haven't heard from her since."

Marcus shook his head and pursed his lips. There was no way Kendall blew off their meeting to have breakfast at a café. *This is bad. Very bad.*

"Did Kendall say who she was meeting, or which café?"

Marcus watched as Selena turned to Cybil and spoke

quietly. *He could tell she knew this was wrong. Very wrong. Kendall was in trouble.*

"No."

"Can you read back exactly what the text message said?" Marcus asked.

"Sure. Hold on a sec. Okay, here it is. 'Hi. I just ran into a friend and we're going to have brunch at a café nearby. Talk later. XOXO.'"

Marcus was silent as fear jolted through him.

"Should I be worried? What time was she supposed to be down there?"

"Maybe. We had an eleven o'clock appointment. It's now twenty after. Selena talked to her earlier, and she was supposed to relay the message to you so that you could join us too."

Silence consumed the line. "She never told me."

Marcus moved the phone away from his mouth and called out to Gates. "How quickly can we get a trace on Kendall's phone?"

"I'll put in the request now."

Luke said, "I'll meet you down at the station." And then the line went dead.

Marcus put his phone in his pocket. "Luke is coming down now. Does your theory indicate Kendall could be in danger?"

Selena held his gaze. "Yes."

Gates hung up the receiver of his desk phone. "Request submitted." Gates looked at Selena. "Do you really think she's in danger?"

"Yes."

"Any way for your people to reach her quicker than my guys can?"

Selena nodded. "No questions asked?"

"No questions."

"I'll make some calls." Selena pulled out her cell phone and hurried toward the hallway. She hunched against the wall and spoke into the phone.

Marcus sat on the edge of Gates's desk. "What was that about?"

"Sometimes you got to work outside the system when it's life or death. If Selena says Kendall is in danger, I trust her," Gates replied.

"You think it's the Howard Davis angle?"

"It would fit. It'll be interesting to find out Selena's theory."

Who was Selena Bailey? And how had she earned Gates's full trust?

Marcus jumped up from the desk. "Kendall's calling!" His heart raced. "Kendall, where have you been?"

A woman's voice answered, "Is this Detective Marcus Rogers?" Marcus's heart sank and shook his head. It was not Kendall calling. He could feel the color draining from his face. "Yes, this is Detective Rogers."

A hush fell over the room.

"This is Officer Donovan. I'm with SFPD, and I'm down at San Francisco General. This phone was found near a person brought in earlier who sustained head trauma from an apparent mugging. Did you say her name is Kendall?"

"Can you describe the woman?" Marcus asked. His knees weakened.

"About five foot six, auburn hair, green eyes. Slight build."

"It sounds like Kendall, Kendall Murphy."

"The one that's been in the news?"

"Yes. That one. How is she?"

"As I said, she sustained a head injury. It's too early to tell. We weren't able to open the phone earlier due to the password protection. Once she was out of surgery, we used the thumbprint to unlock it and figured you'd be the best person to call since you're in law enforcement. Perhaps you know about her family and who to notify."

As Marcus listened to the officer, he scribbled on the whiteboard. *Kendall's been attacked. She's at San Francisco General.*

After a few more details from the officer, he hung up the phone. Everyone stared at him. His gut hadn't been wrong. He knew who did this. "We need to get down to the hospital. They're not sure if she'll make it. Let's head over there now." He eyed Cybil. "Can you notify her grandmother, Janine, and Luke? They'll all want to be there."

Marcus grabbed the keys to their car and rushed out of the station. They had to hurry; at this time of day it could take nearly an hour to get to San Francisco from Ridgemont. Gates followed behind.

Marcus couldn't believe they hadn't acted quicker. After their visit to Bakersfield, he knew something was off. His instinct told him Kendall was in danger. He blamed himself for not getting the deal signed for Dratch quick enough. It was supposed to come in any day, but it didn't matter now if Kendall didn't survive the attack. If she didn't make it, Marcus didn't think he'd ever forgive himself.

CHAPTER THIRTY-ONE

MARCUS

An hour later, Marcus strutted through the automatic doors into San Francisco General Hospital. He and Gates were greeted by the two responding officers. They shook hands and made introductions. Marcus started, "How is she doing? What do we know?"

Officer Donavan, a blonde woman with an athletic build, responded, pulling out and flipping through her notepad. "She got out of surgery about forty-five minutes ago. The surgery was performed to relieve some swelling around her brain. She was struck on the head pretty hard, and the doctor says they aren't sure which way this will go. She could wake up in an hour and be fine. No brain damage. No life-threatening illness. Or it could go the other way. They said that brain injuries are fickle, and he didn't want to speculate on what the outcome would be. He did say, the fact that she's young and healthy is on her side. Now it's essentially a waiting game to see if she wakes up and how much she remembers. It could be a difficult road."

Marcus processed the information. This was his fault. He knew she could be in danger. Yet he didn't do anything to protect her. He should have made sure that there was surveillance on her, or at least around their latest suspect, Howard Davis. Not that they'd known her location, since she was technically in hiding. He tried not to blame himself, but part of him knew that he could've helped avoid this. Sure, he could hide behind the fact that he was following procedure and they didn't have any official evidence against Howard Davis, but his instincts, which is what he'd been following since the beginning of this case, hadn't led him astray yet. He should've warned Kendall.

He asked the officer, "What do we know about the attack?"

Officer Donovan remained serious. "We think she was walking down California Street and was attacked from someone hiding in an alley. He likely pulled her into the less visible area, where he then hit her over the head, likely with a blunt object. The victim cried out, and a passerby on the street heard her and ran over to help."

"Did the witness see anyone standing over her?" Gates asked.

She nodded. "The perpetrator was wearing a ski mask, and he was tall, maybe six foot, and medium build. The perp ran off when the good Samaritan tried to help her. The witness said it all happened very fast."

Marcus processed the information. The description could easily fit Howard Davis or any number of people. "Where's the witness now?"

"He left a little while ago."

"So no way the witness was part of the attack?" Gates asked.

"The witness was pretty shook up. Older guy, I think he may have been in shock, but he refused medical attention. I think he just wanted to go home. He had taken off his shirt to try to stop her bleeding and called 9-1-1. He said he wished he'd gotten a better look, but he was focused on her and not the guy who did it. I believe his statement."

"What makes you think it was a mugging?"

"Because the witness said that the guy had her cell phone in his hand, but when he pushed the guy back the perp dropped the cell phone."

Marcus raised his brows. "You think the perp did this in order to steal her cell phone?"

The cop shrugged and closed her notepad. "She didn't have anything else on her other than a hotel key."

"Do you have a different theory?" the other officer asked.

"It could be related to our case." Marcus turned to Gates. "I think the attacker is the one who sent the text to Luke."

To Marcus, this was looking more and more like the handiwork of Howard Davis. It was not a mugging. The attacker likely texted from Kendall's phone to make sure that nobody would be looking for her, not knowing she had an appointment at the police station. The physical description was a potential match for Howard. Had he found another hitman, or did he attack Kendall himself?

Gates said, "Exactly what I was thinking."

The officer said, "Oh, and by the way, Luke Abbington, the hedge-fund guy, is here in the waiting area. They won't tell him anything because he's not family. Thought you should know. We weren't sure how to handle him. Are they both still suspects?"

Marcus let out a heavy sigh. "Maybe, maybe not. We haven't officially cleared either one of them, but they aren't the only persons of interest."

The officer shifted her weight. "Well, the guy is pretty rattled. I don't know what kind of relationship you have with him, but he's going out of his mind, wanting to know how Kendall is. I'll leave it to you to decide how much to tell him."

Marcus never trusted Luke, but he was fairly confident that Luke would never hurt Kendall. It wouldn't do any harm to let him know what was going on, minus the theory that it wasn't a mugging. *Just in case.* "Where is he at now?"

"Last I saw him, he was over in the waiting room, harassing nurses every other minute."

Marcus said, "I'll talk to him. Thanks for waiting and letting us know what's happening. We'll be in touch."

Marcus and Gates headed toward the waiting room. Luke spotted them approaching and rushed over. "How is she?" He studied them frantically. "You can't possibly think I did this to her! Please, tell me. I'm begging. How is she?"

Marcus read the desperation in Luke's eyes. Like it or not, the man loved her. He filled Luke in on Kendall's current medical status and about the suspected mugging.

Luke's face paled. He stared off into nothing. "I should have gone with her. I should have known she wouldn't have met with a friend."

For the first time, Marcus felt sorry for Luke. The man was devastated. "Luke, it's not your fault."

It was my fault, Marcus thought. He had known about the risk. He should have protected her. He was supposed to be helping Kendall, not getting her killed. "I'm going to ask the nurse if there's any change." Marcus walked over to the nurses' station.

Luke followed closely behind, and Marcus didn't fight him. He had a right to know how Kendall was doing. After all, Marcus was pretty sure Kendall loved Luke.

They both deflated when the nurse said there was no change in Kendall's condition, and she warned that it could be a long wait. From behind, Janine and their grandmother rushed up to the detectives. Janine cried, "Where is she? How is she? What happened?"

Marcus put his hand on her arm. "She got out of surgery an

hour ago. She's not awake yet. We've been told that we don't know how long it will be before she wakes up. "

Janine's eyes filled with tears. "How could this happen?"

Marcus lowered his hand and his gaze and explained what happened. Janine's grandmother and Janine embraced.

Marcus turned back toward the nurse. "This is her grandmother and sister, can they go see her now?"

The nurse nodded and gave them the room number.

Marcus offered to escort them back.

Janine nodded and grabbed her grandmother's hand before following behind Marcus.

When they reached Kendall's room, Grandma and Janine raced to her side. Marcus stared at all the tubes coming out of her nose and mouth. Her head was bandaged, and her face was swollen and bruised. She was barely recognizable.

It was difficult to see a person, who he'd sworn to protect, lying in a hospital bed surrounded by family members broken-hearted over the potential loss. He walked over to Janine. "I'll be in the waiting room if you need anything. You have my number, right?"

Janine nodded.

He silently exited the room.

By the time he reached the waiting room, the group of Kendall's supporters had grown. Cybil and Selena both joined Luke and Gates. By the blank stares and shaking heads, Marcus knew they'd gotten the most up-to-date information.

He approached. "Since they don't know when she'll wake up, what do you say we go over the theory you'd come to present at the station. I have a feeling it matches mine." He knew the best way to help Kendall now was to capture her attacker and husband's killer—and bring him to justice.

Selena said, "Yes, I brought my laptop. Huddle around, and I can show you what I've been working on."

Marcus and the group crowded around Selena, who sat with her laptop propped on her thighs.

After finishing her presentation, explaining her theory as fast as humanly possible, Selena said, "Based on phone records, video coverage, and both of their financials, which contain no irregularities or suspicious activity, you can see there was absolutely no contact between Luke and Kendall in the last year, prior to their meeting in the middle of May. And no contact between either of them with Irwin Dratch. Using the same type of analysis, we found one person with suspicious irregularities in financials and a suspected sighting with Dratch. The video isn't great, but it shows a man meeting with Dratch a few weeks before George's death. That man matches the height, build, and gait of the person with financial irregularities, and he has an actual motive. That person is Howard Davis. He stands to inherit everything from his mother if both George and Kendall are gone."

I fucking knew it. Damn, she was good, Marcus thought.

Selena said, "Oh, if I didn't mention this before, don't ask us how we got this information."

Marcus was already pretty confident Selena's team had taken illegal measures to obtain this information so quickly. There was no way any of it could be presented in a court of law. However, it could give them some timelines to go back and request surveillance cameras legally, and then use that information to build their case.

Marcus explained, "We had the same suspicions. When we questioned him last week, Eleanor Davis's lawyer stopped by and disclosed that Kendall was named in the will. Howard Davis was visibly surprised by the revelation."

Selena said, "That is why he acted against Kendall now. Chances are if he'd known earlier, it wouldn't have been just George who was killed last year. It would've been both of them.

Gates said, "Nice work. One little problem. We still don't have any evidence that we could use in court, or even to get an arrest warrant."

Marcus's blood pressure rose. "Where the hell is that deal we were trying to strike with Dratch? If he names Howard, we can arrest him right now."

"True, but we don't need to arrest Howard if we can get him in for questioning. I'll call Bakersfield PD and have them pick him up. If he refuses to come down to the station, at least the locals will have an eye on him. Assuming he's there. But based on today's actions, he may not be at home; he may be right here in San Francisco. I'll put out an APB on him in both Bakersfield and San Francisco. While I do that, Marcus, you work with Selena to create a plan to see if any of the evidence can be salvaged for an arrest warrant."

Marcus nodded and took a seat next to Selena, forcing himself to focus on the case and not the fruity scent of her shampoo.

He needed to get this guy if it was the last thing he did. But how? Sure, Selena's evidence was damming, but not bullet-proof. He had a feeling the only way they were going to nail the coffin shut on Howard Davis was to get Dratch to identify him. Where the hell was that deal?

CHAPTER THIRTY-TWO

MARCUS

Marcus set down his phone on his desk. *Damn*. No change in Kendall's condition. Not only was he concerned about her well-being, but he also was hoping for any information about her attacker that could be used as evidence. He glanced up as Gates approached, wearing a frown on his face. "Bad news, buddy. They can't find Howard Davis. Bakersfield PD went to his house, and he's not there. They talked to the neighbors and found out the mother was rushed to the hospital a few days ago. They hadn't seen either one of them since. So the officers went down to the hospital where his mother was supposed to be. Mom's there. Howard's not. There was some staff turnover, which means they can't be sure if anybody ever saw Howard at the hospital. In the last forty-eight hours, Howard could have driven up to San Francisco and attacked Kendall or planned the attack on Kendall. I called in my buddies over at SFPD. They're on high alert and actively looking for anyone fitting Howard's description. If they find him, they won't reveal he's a suspect, but they'll let him know we have more questions. Considering we still don't have any usable evidence yet, it's the best we can do."

Marcus tried to interject, but Gates hushed him. "Yes, I already have a uniform on Kendall's hospital room. Plus, she's there with her grandma and sister. She should be safe for now."

Marcus sat back. She was safe in the hospital. Howard Davis didn't exactly seem like a mastermind who'd be able to get around a guard and two other civilians, but Marcus had assumed wrong before. If Howard had gone this long without suspicion, maybe Marcus needed to give him more credit.

Should he reach out to Selena Bailey, the private investigator who seem to have magical powers when it came to obtaining video surveillance? He didn't like the idea of using back channels, but in this event, it could save Kendall's life. Maybe it would be worth it. Gates seemed to think Selena's help was okay when they were looking for Kendall, how about now?

Gates said, "That was the bad news, buddy. Are you ready for some good news?"

Marcus straightened. "What good news?"

Gates slapped down a folder on his desk. Marcus flipped open the cover and skimmed through the pages outlining the deal the district attorney had made with Irwin Dratch. Before Marcus spoke, Gates said, "Already called his lawyer."

Adrenaline soaring through his veins, Marcus shot up from his seat. "Let's go talk to Dratch." *This is it. The moment of truth.* They would get a definitive answer, and the information would stand up in court.

Thirty minutes later, the detectives entered the conference room. Dratch and his lawyer sat behind the table. Dratch had a smirk on his face that Marcus didn't like. *Yes, the jerk got a helluva deal, and he knows it.*

Gates pulled out a seat and slid down onto it. He leaned over and pushed the papers in front of Dratch's lawyer and said, "It's all there in writing."

Marcus stared at Irwin Dratch and demanded, "Talk."

His lawyer raised a single hand. "One moment, please. I need to review this to ensure we're in agreement with the deal. Patience *is* a virtue, Detective."

Dratch teased, "Yes, we must make sure the details are just right."

Marcus wanted to punch Dratch in the face. He was taunting them. It made Marcus's blood boil.

The lawyer said, "Okay, says here you're bringing the charges down from first-degree murder to manslaughter, plus the other charges. Fifteen years in a minimum-security prison. I believe that's acceptable, right Irwin?"

Irwin nodded. "It's acceptable."

"All right, now that we have that out of the way, who hired you to kill George Davis?" Marcus asked, body vibrating.

Dratch adjusted his position on the chair and sat up straight. He seemed to be feigning a look of innocence. "Well, I didn't know his name, but we did meet a few times."

You didn't know his name? Marcus wanted to pounce on him. Gates placed his hand on Marcus's arm, as if to keep him in place.

Gates said, "Why don't you start from the beginning. The when, the where, the details you do know."

Irwin relaxed into the seat and told his tale. "A month before George's death, I was put into contact with my employer. That's what he wanted me to call him - employer. We met and discussed terms. We met a second time, in the same place, and I received my down payment, then I committed to the task at hand. I communicated the completion of the task through a burner phone. That's when we set up a time and place for the final payment."

Marcus had lost all patience for Irwin Dratch. His slow, detail-less story had snapped his last nerve. He raised his voice.

"The terms of the deal require you to give information that leads to the arrest of the person who hired you. If you can't identify him, the deal is null and void."

Dratch said, smiling, "Calm down, detective. I can give you a description. I'm good with faces."

Marcus spat. "You better have a photographic memory, or we walk out of here with that deal."

"It's lucky that I have a pretty damn good memory. Get your sketch artist."

Marcus glanced at Gates and shook his head before standing up and kicking his chair out of the way and exiting the room.

MARCUS WAS ABOUT TO BLOW A FUSE. "WHAT WAS THAT? No fucking name?"

"Look, if the sketch is close enough to Howard Davis, we'll show Dratch a photo and catch us a positive ID. I think we'll get what we need. Now, we need to get that sketch artist down here. I might be able to exchange some favors to get her here fast." Gates glanced up from the phone on his desk. "Buddy, you need to cool your jets."

Marcus couldn't believe Irwin Dratch was dicking them around, although he shouldn't have been surprised, considering he was a freaking hitman. Gates was right again. *Damn.* He needed to calm down so they could apprehend Howard Davis and put him away for the rest of his life, and not in some country club prison, that's for damn sure.

THEY RETURNED TO THE CONFERENCE ROOM WITH THE

sketch artist, Laney Burke, one of the best in the area. After introductions, Marcus leaned up against the wall as Laney sat across from Dratch. He had too much energy bottled up to sit across from that piece of trash.

Gates said, "Before we start with Laney, let's get a few other characteristics down, like height, weight, ethnicity, hair color, and eye color."

"About six feet. Dark hair. Dark eyes. Caucasian. Not skinny, about medium build, a bit of a paunch."

"Is that a good start for you?" Gates asked the artist.

"Yeah, that's good. I'll take it from here. Thanks, Detective."

Gates joined Marcus over at the wall. They watched as Laney asked detailed questions about the facial structure, shape, nose, chin, and other distinguishing features.

The detectives spoke to each other in hushed tones. Gates said, "That sounds a lot like Howard Davis."

"I'd bet money on it."

"Any word on how Kendall's doing?"

"No change."

Gates peered over at Laney's sketch. "I think it's him. We should talk about strategy. As soon as we get the positive ID, we'll alert BPD and SFPD to scour their respective areas and have him arrested. You know, chances are he doesn't know she's still alive."

Marcus rose off the wall. "We could put out a release saying she died. Maybe smoke him out?"

"Buddy, that's not a bad idea. If we hold a funeral, he has to show up, right?"

"He is her brother-in-law."

"This could work. Except, what if she doesn't make it? Right now, the family is fearing the worst. Faking her death may break them."

Gates was right. They could catch the guy, but at what cost?

The family had been through so much already. George's death. Kendall's attack. Being scrutinized by the press. Having to go into hiding. They'd been through enough.

Laney called over to the detectives. "I think we're done."

Gates and Marcus scurried over. Marcus glanced down at the sketch. It was the spitting image of Howard Davis. He knew it. They were going to catch this guy. He would get justice for George and Kendall.

Marcus looked over at Irwin Dratch and raised the sketch. "Is this the guy who hired you to kill George Davis?"

Irwin grinned. "Yes, sir. That's the man who hired me."

Gates said, "Based on the sketch, we have some photos for you to look at. If one of the photos is the man who hired you, you tell us. Can you do that?"

With a Cheshire-cat smile, Dratch said, "Of course, detectives. I'm here to help."

Marcus wanted to smack the smug look right off his face. Dratch was a career murderer who would spend only fifteen years in a minimum-security prison. It was disgusting, but it was necessary in order to put not one, but two bad guys away. Marcus understood that now.

THEY STOOD OVER DRATCH AS HE STUDIED THE ARRAY OF images. Using his pointer finger, Dratch tapped the photo of Howard Davis. "That's your guy. Hey, uh, what's his name anyway?"

Marcus thought it was odd that Dratch wanted to know his name. Why?

Gates explained. "Howard Davis—George's brother."

"Cain and Abel," Dratch commented.

Dratch's lawyer grimaced. "Are we done here?"

Gates said, "Yes, we are."

Marcus and Gates exited the room. Gates said, "Now to find that motherfucker."

Marcus's thoughts exactly—and before it was too late.

CHAPTER THIRTY-THREE

KENDALL

KENDALL'S EYELIDS FLUTTERED BEFORE OPENING FULLY. Her tired eyes swam around the hospital room. She tilted her head toward Janine, who was hunched over her laptop, sitting crisscrossed on a large cushioned chair next to her bed. In a gravelly voice Kendall hardly recognized, she called out, "Janine."

Kendall watched as her sister flustered about, setting aside her things and shooting out of her chair. She scurried over to the bed and took Kendall's hand in hers. Her younger sister's eyes were bloodshot with dark circles underneath. When was the last time her sister had slept? Janine exclaimed, "You're awake!"

Kendall was obviously in a hospital room, but she didn't know why. She swallowed, and her throat burned. She said, "What happened? Why am I here?"

"You had an accident, which left you with a head injury. I'll tell you more details in a second. I need to call the nurse first; they said to call them as soon as you woke up." Janine grabbed the remote and pressed the call button to notify the nurse. "How are you feeling?"

Kendall spoke slowly. "I'm tired. My head hurts. Throat hurts. What happened? Why am I here?"

"When you were out for a walk, someone hit you over the head. They think it was a mugging. Some stranger came to your rescue, called 9-1-1, and then you were rushed to the hospital."

"When?" Kendall didn't remember going on a walk.

"Two days ago."

I've been here for two days? Two days erased from her life. It was unsettling. At the sound of footsteps and rustling fabric, Kendall glanced to the left. A nurse in rose-colored scrubs approached, wearing a jangling necklace and a bright smile. "Well, hello! It's great to see you awake. I'm Danica, one of your nurses. Do you know who and where you are?"

How bad were her injuries if the first thing they ask is if she knew who she was? "I'm Kendall Murphy, and I'm in a hospital. My sister filled me in about the why."

"It's nice to finally meet you, Kendall. You had us worried for a while."

"Why? How bad is it?" She didn't feel like she was dying. But then again, she didn't know how it felt to be dying.

"You've been in a coma, but I'll let the doctor explain everything else. He'll be here soon to examine you. But know that we're all very happy you're awake. Can I get you anything? Are you thirsty?"

Kendall swallowed again. "Yeah, maybe some water."

The nurse chimed, "One water, coming right up. Janine, honey, do you need anything?"

Janine shook her head and said to Kendall, "I'm so happy you're awake. I thought we were going to lose you that first day . . ."

Kendall watched as her sister's lower lip quivered. "No need to worry. It'll take more than a little bump on the head to get me out of the game."

Janine laughed through tears. "Oh, Kendall. What would we do without you?"

"Not sure, but you look terrible. Have you slept?"

"Thanks, sis," Janine teased. "I've been here ever since you got out of surgery. By the way, you had surgery—to reduce the swelling. I didn't want to leave your side in case you woke up."

Kendall's heart swelled. She was so lucky to have her little sister. Grandma and Janine were the only family she had left. An image of Luke floated across her brain. "Has anyone talked to Luke? Has he come by?"

Janine smirked playfully. "Don't worry. Mr. Prince Charming has been here nonstop, but they won't let him in because he isn't family. We've been giving him updates. He's dying to see you. Actually, I should go call him and Grandma. I wouldn't want to be on the wrong side of either of them."

Before Kendall could respond, a doctor in blue scrubs and a white coat, with a stethoscope draped around his neck, entered. "Kendall, it's true. You're awake." He smiled, holding a clipboard in his hands. "Great to see you."

He approached the bed. "How are you feeling?"

"Headache. Sore throat. Tired. Really tired."

He nodded. "From one to ten, how would you categorize your headache pain? Ten being a knife going through your skull and one, a mild ache."

That's a vivid description. Yikes. "Maybe a five?"

He winked. "Great."

Is it great?

"Perfectly normal. We'll up your meds a bit to make you more comfortable. Has anybody explained to you the extent of your injuries?"

Janine answered for her. "I let her know she had a brain injury, and that she had surgery to reduce the swelling. But that's it."

The doctor said, "That's correct. You had what we call a traumatic brain injury. With these types of injuries, there's always the possibility of memory loss, motor function issues, and cognitive discrepancies. When a patient wakes up within forty-eight hours of the event, it's a very good sign. The fact you're awake and having conversations is fantastic. It makes me hopeful, but I would like to get some tests started right away. Is that okay with you, Kendall?"

Do I have a choice? "That's fine."

Janine said, "I'll call Luke and Grandma."

Kendall lifted her fingers to wave. *Now for tests. Fun.*

JANINE RETURNED TO THE ROOM AS THE DOCTOR WAS finishing the exam. She asked, "Is everything okay?"

The doctor turned around. "So far, everything is looking really good. I didn't identify any memory loss or any cognitive issues. But we'll run a few more tests over the next couple of days to be sure."

Janine threw her hand over her chest, and tears streamed down her face. "I'm so happy to hear that." She leaned over and wrapped her arm across Kendall.

Kendall said, "Oh, Janine, I'm not going anywhere." She looked over at the doctor. "Are we done with the exam?"

"Yep, you're all done. Do you have any questions?"

"Can I get up and walk around?"

"Not quite. You need to take it easy. You haven't been upright in a while, so we'll bring the nurse in here to prop you up, and if you're feeling good enough, we can get you into a wheelchair if you'd like to leave the room. We'll see how that goes and decide when you're ready for walking. Sometimes our bodies have a slower response than we'd like. Your body has been through a lot. We want to make sure you stay healthy and don't do anything to impede your recovery. Any other questions?"

"No. Thank you."

"My pleasure. Take care."

She nodded and waved as he exited.

Janine said, "I called Grandma and Luke. They both will be here as soon as they can. I wasn't sure if you wanted me to call Detective Hottie or not? Or your lawyer?"

Kendall thought about that for a moment. Marcus had totally iced her out. She couldn't believe he thought she'd killed George. Maybe she shouldn't be so hard on him. He was just doing his job. What about her lawyer? Selena?

Janine seemed to pick up on her hesitation to speak with any of these people. "Your lawyer, your private investigator, Selena, and the detective have been calling to check on you several times a day. They're all very worried. I can call them or wait for them to call. Your decision."

She wondered what had happened with the case. She said, yawning, "It's fine. You can call them. I'm so tired. With all this lying around, you'd think I'd be fully charged."

Janine reminded her. "You heard the doctor. You experienced a traumatic physical injury. Your body needs time to heal itself. You'll probably be tired for a while."

"That sucks."

Janine giggled. "Yeah, it does suck."

The sound of footsteps rushing toward her bed startled her, and then a grin crept up her face. "Luke."

His eyes sparkled. "Oh, Kendall, I'm so happy to see you. My God, I was going out of my mind. How are you? How do you feel?" He traced his finger along the side of her face as he waited for her response, before gently placing her hand in his.

"I'll be okay."

"Is it okay if I kiss you, or will it hurt?"

"I'll take the chance."

Luke leaned over and brushed her lips lightly with his own. She briefly closed her eyes and then opened them as he leaned back.

Janine called from the other side of the bed. "I'll head out to the waiting room and wait for Grandma to give you guys a little bit of privacy, but the nurse is coming back soon, so you might want to keep your clothes on."

Kendall smiled. "I'll try my best." Like she had the energy to take off her shirt, let alone get jiggy with Luke. Nonetheless, she would be perfectly happy with him holding her hand and giving her light kisses for as long as he was willing.

Luke beamed down at her. "I'm glad you still have your sense of humor."

"I'm still me, just in a hospital bed."

Luke lowered his head. "I was so worried. I don't know what I would've done if I lost you too. It was the worst feeling."

Kendall watched as tears fell from his eyes like tiny raindrops. She squeezed his hand. "You didn't lose me, Luke. I'm right here."

He wiped his eyes with his free hand and looked back at her. "And for that, I will be eternally grateful."

The reunion was interrupted by the nurse returning to sit her up. "You're looking a bit more cheerful since I was in here last. I have a feeling it has something to do with this gentleman here."

Kendall could feel herself blushing. "This is Luke."

"Hi, Luke, nice to meet you. Kendall, I'll only be a minute. I have a few procedures to perform. So . . ."

"I can step out if you'd like," Luke said.

Would the "procedures" be embarrassing? She wasn't sure she was ready for that next step in the relationship. She said, "Give us a few minutes?"

"Anything for you."

As Luke left, the nurse said, "Boyfriend? Husband?"

"Boyfriend."

"That man is in love. I wouldn't be surprised at your next checkup if he's been promoted to husband. This will take just a few minutes, and then you can get back to Mr. Tall, Dark, and Handsome."

Husband? She was too tired to think about that.

THE NEXT MORNING, KENDALL WOKE TO THE SOUND OF heavy footsteps. A sleepy smile formed on her face. "Back already?"

She opened her eyes and flinched.

"Hello, Kendall."

The lilt in her name. That voice. Her mind flashed back to the street that morning—before it had all gone dark.

CHAPTER THIRTY-FOUR

KENDALL

KENDALL GRABBED FOR THE RED CALL BUTTON, BUT Howard snatched it away before she had the chance. He sneered, "What's the matter, Kendall, not happy to see me?"

Why had he attacked her? What was happening? She said, "Luke will be back any minute." She remembered the guard. Where was the guard? Her hands shook.

Howard edged closer. "Oh, right. Luke, the man you used to replace my brother. Too bad your happiness will be short-lived. You know," he narrowed his eyes, "I never did like you much. What did George ever see in you? You're a bit plain for my taste. Boring, really."

His words stung, sizzling with the fear coursing through her body. If she screamed out, would he be able to attack her before anyone could hear? She scowled, putting on a brave face. "I think the feeling is mutual. Love the new look, by the way. Who are you trying to be? George? You'll never be like George. He was smart, successful, funny, and sweet." She shut her eyes in an attempt to block the tears from falling. George had been all of those things. She shook her head, taking in a deep breath.

Howard's face turned crimson.

She'd hit a nerve. *Was that good or bad?*

Kendall glanced around the room. What could she use to create some noise and get somebody's attention before it was too late?

He spat, "I'm a bit more alive-looking, don't you think? I admit, I do think the blond suits me, don't you? You know what they say, blonds have more fun. And Kendall, I'm having a blast." He snickered.

"Why are you here?" She'd never liked Howard. He gave her the heebie-jeebies every time they met. She'd also sensed a darkness in him, but never would have taken him for somebody who would physically harm her. Why had he? Why would he do this? Did he kill George, too?

"Yes, I figured you'd be wondering that. Why *am* I here? Why are any of us here, Kendall? But to answer your question, I'm here to say goodbye."

She didn't like the sound of that. She needed to act fast. "Are you going somewhere?" Her chest tightened.

"Oh, I'm sorry, I wasn't clear. I'm not the one going anywhere, dear sweet sister."

The way he said *sister* was vile. He was vile. She heard a faint shuffling of shoes. Was someone coming? Or was it the drugs she was on? She looked Howard up and down. He didn't appear to have any obvious weapons. Could she stand and walk on her own? She hadn't tried yet. Doctor's orders. But she had a feeling it was now or never.

In one swoop, she swung her legs off the bed, steadying herself with her hands on the bed. Now lightheaded, she screamed, "Help!" Her voice was weak. She tried to run, but her legs buckled, and she tumbled to the floor, yanking the IV from her arm. She yelled out in pain.

Howard growled. "I see you're going to do this the hard

way." He dashed over to where she lay and wrapped his thick fingers around her neck and began to squeeze.

She tried to holler, but no sound escaped her mouth. She flailed her arms in an attempt to claw at Howard. If nothing else, she'd have his DNA under her fingernails. He wouldn't get away with this.

She couldn't breathe.

She couldn't scream.

A sound like fireworks rang in her ears. Howard's hands released her as he fell back. She put her hands to her neck and heaved as she tried to regain her breath. Her throat was on fire.

She glanced forward. A flash of feet and legs running toward Howard, who was lying on the ground, startled her. Howard's blood seeped onto the tile, but he was still moving.

From behind, an arm swooped around her. "Are you okay?" She stared up at Luke and nodded. He held her tight and yelled. "Nurse! Doctor!"

She heard a familiar voice. "I'll get help." *Was that Detective Gates?*

Her breathing steadied, and she looked back up at Luke and gave a weak smile. "I'm so happy to see you."

He hugged her tight. "I'm so sorry I left you." He pulled back. "I'm so sorry. Let's get you off of the floor."

He lifted her up and carried her over to the bed and placed her down gently. "Are you sure you're okay? Where does it hurt?"

"What's going on? Where is he?"

Luke peered over his shoulder. "Don't worry about that right now, sweetheart, let's get you taken care of."

She strained to see Detective Rogers on his knees, hand-cuffing Howard, who lay on the floor with blood oozing from his shoulder. Detective Gates rushed back in the room and helped Marcus pull her brother-in-law to his feet. Howard yelled obscenities and demanded medical attention. The detectives ignored his rant.

Detective Rogers pushed him forward and said, "Howard Davis, you are under arrest for the conspiracy to commit the murder of George Davis and attempted murder of Kendall Murphy. You have the right to remain silent . . ."

Kendall stared in disbelief as Detective Rogers read Howard his Miranda rights. Howard had hired Irwin Dratch to kill George. Why? Had he hated his brother that much?

The detectives didn't speak to either her or Luke as they escorted Howard out of her hospital room.

She clung to Luke as the doctors and nurses rushed in. He kissed her forehead and unwrapped her arms before stepping back and letting the professionals take over.

CHAPTER THIRTY-FIVE

MARCUS

Marcus's heart warmed at the sound of laughter radiating from Kendall's hospital room. It would have destroyed him if he had not been able to save her or find the person responsible for her husband's death. He was lucky this time. He understood that now. In the future, he needed to make sure he kept a wider distance between his victims and his investigations. He had grown to care for Kendall and her family. He was fortunate this case had a happy ending. He vowed to never again make promises he wasn't sure he could keep.

Marcus entered the room and stopped at the edge of Kendall's bed. Not surprising, Luke was on one side of her and Janine on the other. Despite the bruising on her neck from Howard's fierce grip and residual facial swelling from the original attack, she appeared in decent shape. He said, "Hi there."

Her guardians turned to stare at him. He said, sheepishly, "I hate to break up the party."

Kendall grinned. "Not a problem. Janine was amusing us with one of her antics."

"How are you feeling?"

"A lot better. Just a little stir-crazy. I'm looking forward to breaking out of this joint. I miss walking and being able to make a pot of coffee. I didn't realize how precious mobility and life was until I almost lost it all. Life is definitely worth living, and I'm grateful for each moment."

She's definitely in good spirits. And happy. "Did they say when you'll be discharged?"

"Not yet. Hopefully soon. Unfortunately, the episode yesterday, Howard trying to kill me and all, may have delayed it a bit."

Marcus's heart sank. As soon as he'd heard that the officer had been called away to an urgent matter, he'd rushed to her hospital room. He hated to think about what would've happened if he hadn't already been in the hospital, or if he'd been two minutes later.

"I hope it's soon, too. I hate to do this here, but I was hoping to take your official statement from yesterday's incident, as well as discuss the details of the original attack on the street. Everything happened so fast, we didn't get a chance to get any statements or connect the two attacks."

Kendall nodded. "Yeah, sure, now is fine. Should they stay or should they go?" She motioned at Luke and Janine. "Does it matter?"

"It's up to you." Marcus watched as Luke and Kendall kept their hands locked together. He understood. If he were in Luke's position, he wouldn't ever want to leave her side again either. Seeing the two of them together, relaxed and happy, sharing stolen glances; it was obvious they were in love. He cleared his thoughts. *The case.* "May we get started? Do you remember anything about the attack on Monday morning?"

"Yes. It was Howard, I knew it when he came into the room yesterday. His voice, the way he says my name, it's creepy. It's the same way the attacker said it."

"I'm sorry. I'm not following what you mean. Can you start from the beginning?"

"I was walking on the street and somebody called my name. They said 'Kendall,' and I turned because I recognized the voice, but it came from someone in a black ski mask. That's pretty much all I remember before it went black. The voice, it was Howard's. I'm certain."

Marcus wondered why Howard decided to attack Kendall on his own. Perhaps it was his mother's failing health that made him panic. Maybe he didn't have enough time to hire a hitman to kill Kendall and get her name removed from the will. He'd become desperate. Desperation ruins the ability to think clearly and rationally. Luckily, Howard's two attempts on Kendall's life weren't successful. He asked, "Do you remember anything else?"

"Nothing. I still don't understand why he attacked me. I heard you arrest him for George's murder. Did he hire Irwin Dratch? Did he hate George that much that he wanted to kill him and me?"

Marcus looked at Luke and Janine. He was surprised they hadn't explained what was going on. Or her lawyer or Selena.

Marcus nodded. "He's refusing to talk to us right now, but our theory is that yes, he hired Dratch to kill George. Eleanor Davis, George and Howard's mother, your mother-in-law, had named you, George, and Howard in her will. We think Howard took out a hit on George to remove his name from the will. What Howard didn't know at the time, and didn't find out until very recently, was that you were named in the will too. He had thought it was just George and him. Eleanor Davis is not doing well and may only have one or two weeks left before she passes. We think Howard got desperate and needed to take you out of the equation, and fast. So," he raised his brows, "essentially, the motive was greed. I'm not sure if you are aware of the size of Eleanor Davis's estate. What I will say is that it's considerable."

Kendall's face looked confused. "No, I didn't know. I mean, I didn't think that she was poor, or without money, but I had no idea. I guess it makes sense. She did pay for George's schooling and several attempts at getting Howard to attend college or fund his latest donkey-brained business idea. How big is considerable? Like, how much is worth killing your family for? I can't even imagine."

"For some, it's far less than you'd expect. But, for Howard it was . . ." He paused. "I'm not sure if you want me to disclose, with people around, considering you'll inherit half of her estate."

Kendall remained focused on Marcus. "You can speak freely in front of them."

"Howard's price was roughly twenty million."

Kendall's mouth dropped open. "Twenty million? She lives in that dinky little house. How on earth is she worth twenty million?"

Marcus could tell she wasn't faking her surprise. Kendall had no idea of the fortune that her mother-in-law was sitting on. "Apparently, she had family money, as well as a sizable inheritance and life insurance from when Mr. Davis, George Davis, Sr., passed away."

Kendall said, "So, half—ten million—wasn't enough? He doesn't have a penny to his name, and he felt like he needed to kill us for the extra ten million?" Kendall grimaced. "What a jabroni. I never liked him."

Janine and Luke snickered. He hadn't taken Kendall for an *Always Sunny* fan. Maybe the pain meds were making her loopy. She wasn't usually so colorful. Maybe it was the new Kendall? Near-death experiences tended to change a person. Or maybe this was what Kendall was like in her natural state. Since they'd met, Kendall's state of mind had ranged from devastation to anger to sadness to terrified.

Marcus said, "You never know, maybe he felt you guys didn't deserve any of the money. Maybe it was greed mixed with resentment for having to take care of his mother."

"So, what is going on with the case? I feel like I've been in a black hole for the last four days. Has it really only been four days? It feels like forever."

Here it goes. "Irwin Dratch made a deal and will be serving fifteen years in a minimum-security prison."

"Only fifteen years? In a minimum-security prison? Is it just me or is that crazy? He killed George!" She looked over at Luke. "Crazy, right?"

Luke said, "Absolutely."

Marcus had a feeling this was how she'd react. It was ludicrous that a hitman would only receive fifteen years in prison, after killing God only knows how many people. He said, "It was the only way we could get him to talk. He identified Howard as the man who hired him. Without Dratch's testimony, we didn't have any usable evidence against Howard, despite all of the unofficial, circumstantial evidence provided by Selena. It was the only way we could arrest Howard. The DA felt that arresting Howard was more important than additional sentencing for Dratch. Dratch is fifty-five and will be spending his golden years in prison. When he gets out, he'll be seventy, an old man, if he doesn't die in prison first. We're assuming that at seventy, he won't be much of a threat. And it's likely he'll get charged with unrelated crimes that they've now linked him to. So, he may never get out."

Based on Kendall's expression, Marcus didn't think Kendall agreed. He supposed he could understand that. The man who killed her husband still had a life to look forward to.

"What about Howard? How many years will he get?" Kendall asked.

Marcus said, "He's going away for, most likely, the rest of his life."

"You think he'll get life?"

"Depends. The district attorney may try to get him to take a plea to avoid a costly trial, but they'll likely prosecute pretty hard on this one."

Kendall seemed to sink into her hospital bed. She said, "All of this still seems unreal."

"I can see how that could be. If you're ready, I can take your statement about what happened yesterday with Howard."

"Sure, now's fine."

She explained to Marcus all the details of the events that happened prior to Marcus, Gates, and Luke rushing into her hospital room. When she was finished, he flipped his notepad closed and tucked it into the inside pocket of his blazer. "All right, I think I have everything I need."

Kendall said, "Wait, don't go yet. There are some things I'd like to say." He halted his steps. "First of all, thank you, Marcus. You promised me, on that first day we met, you would find out who did this to George. And you kept your promise. Thank you."

The others echoed her sentiment.

He was touched by the sight of her eyes filling with tears. He said, "You're very welcome. But I was just doing my job. And to be honest, we probably would've eventually gotten him, but we got him quicker because of Selena. Be sure to thank her. Have you talked to her?" He wondered if he would ever see Selena Bailey again. He wanted to express his gratitude to her too—or was it more than that?

Kendall said, "Yes, she promised to come by later."

Why was he suddenly disappointed that he'd miss her?

Was he really going to say this? *Yes. She needs to hear it.* "Kendall, I'm sorry for how I treated you once you became a person of interest. For what it's worth, I never believed you had anything to do with this. Please know that it was the job. But I wanted you to know that. I never ever thought you were guilty."

She nodded in acknowledgment. "I appreciate it."

"Okay, and I'm really going now. With this wrapped up, Gates and I caught a couple of new cases. Busy. Busy. Take care."

"You too, and maybe get some sleep."

He smiled. "I'll try."

He waved as he exited Kendall's hospital room. It felt good to have closed his first big case. Not only had it put a shiny star on his career, but now he'd be freed up to look into his brother's case and maybe even get one of those 'lives' Gates kept hounding him about.

CHAPTER THIRTY-SIX

KENDALL

Kendall listened intently to her doctor's orders. "Does that mean I can go home soon?"

"As of right now, I think we'll be able to discharge you on Monday."

Kendall relaxed into her hospital bed. She was so tired of sitting in that bed. Friends and family had visited constantly and offered to take her around in a wheelchair, but she was tired of these hospital walls. She couldn't wait to leave. But where would she go? She'd been staying in a hotel. Did she want to go back to her old house? That was easy to decide. No.

"Monday can't come fast enough."

The doctor continued, "Do you have someone to stay with you once you're discharged?"

"Why does someone need to stay with me?"

"Brain injuries can be tricky. Sometimes symptoms manifest later than you'd expect. It's best to have someone around in case the unexpected happens."

That's crappy. Not in the clear yet. Who could she stay with? She glanced over at Janine.

Her little sister said, "You can stay with me in my new

apartment. It's small and filled with boxes, but I can get it ready by the time you're discharged."

"Are you sure?"

Janine shook her head. "You don't even have to ask. Of course! I've got a great view. It's probably good for recovery. I can probably take more time off from work to take care of you. It'll be fun. I promise." Kendall thought her sister's smile was forced. Janine had been so excited about living on her own for the first time, Kendall hated the idea of imposing.

Luke stood up from his seat. "This is silly. Janine, Kendall can stay with me. I'll take time off work. I'll be around all of the time to make sure you take your medication and have whatever you need or want."

"Luke, that's so sweet, but I can't ask you to do that."

Janine added, "Yeah, plus, it's totally fine. She can stay with me."

"Let's think about this rationally, ladies. Janine, I'm sure you would take wonderful care of your sister, but you're new at your job and probably haven't accrued much vacation time. And you haven't really moved into your apartment yet. It might be better for you to go back to work and focus on setting up your new place. I, on the other hand, have tons of vacation time. I have a lovely guest room that Kendall is welcome to stay in. It will be my pleasure to take care of you, sweetheart."

Guest room?

Janine raised her eyebrow, she must have been thinking what Kendall was thinking.

But, Luke was right, and if Kendall was being honest with herself, she absolutely wanted to stay with him. But was it too soon? What was holding her back? The only other man she'd lived with was George. *George.*

Luke said, "I see the hamster wheel spinning."

Kendall said, "Okay, I'll stay with you, *during* my recovery."

Luke bent over to kiss her on the lips. "Good."

The doctor said, "Well, it appears as if you'll be in good hands. Keep up the good work."

Kendall waved as the doctor left.

She glanced back up at Luke. "Thank you for agreeing to take care of me."

He brushed the hair from her face and tucked it behind her ear. "It's my pleasure."

Janine said, "Okay, I can tell when three's a crowd. Kendall, I'll see you tomorrow?"

Kendall grinned and winked at Luke.

"Bye, Janine. Drive safe." Luke waved.

Was it really all going to be over in a few days? Out of the hospital and no longer a murder suspect or dating a murder suspect. *I definitely like the sound of that. Oh, the things I never thought I'd say.*

Kendall reached up to pull Luke closer. "Can I get a kiss?"

"Yes. And for the record, the answer is always yes."

His soft lips on hers made her body feel weightless. He flicked her lips with the tip of his tongue, and her body tensed. Even in a hospital bed, he could send electricity through her. She couldn't wait to get out of the wretched hospital. The sounds of footsteps ended their mini make-out.

Selena stopped at the end of the bed. "Am I interrupting something? I can come back."

Kendall put her fingers to her lips, savoring the last bit of Luke before answering. "Oh no, stay. We were just celebrating some good news."

Selena smiled brightly. "Do tell."

"I'm busting out of here on Monday!"

"Congratulations. Are you feeling a lot better?"

Kendall nodded. "I'm feeling so much better. The headaches have decreased in intensity, which is nice. I'm still a bit tired, but the doctors are confident I'll regain my strength, and the headaches will subside completely as long as I rest and take it easy for a while."

"That's great news."

"I hear *thanks* is in order. Detective Rogers was here earlier and explained what you did to help. Thank you, Selena. You're amazing. I've been in awe of you ever since we met. I'm so grateful that Cybil put us in contact and that you were able to find closure for us and clear our names. You have my deepest gratitude."

Luke said, "Yes, Selena, you and your team were amazing. We'll forever be in your debt."

Selena's cheeks turned pink. "That isn't necessary. I was just doing my job."

Kendall didn't buy it. Selena had been so attentive and personable throughout the whole experience. She'd been delicate when it came to news about Luke and had given her sage advice while she worked non-stop to solve the case. Selena was a rock star.

The room fell quiet.

Kendall had asked Selena to visit to discuss some other matters as well. She turned to Luke. "Do you mind if we have a few minutes?"

Luke paused before answering. "Sure. I'll be in the cafeteria. Text me when you want me to come back, okay?" He gave her a quick peck before leaving.

She saw the concern in his eyes when she asked him to leave the room. She hated to worry him, but this was something she needed to do, without him.

Kendall said, "Please, sit."

Selena sat in the chair beside the bed. "You two seem to be doing well."

Kendall nodded.

"I assume you still want the background on him, and that's why you wanted him to leave?"

"Partly. I trust him, but wonder if I can trust my own instincts. I'm not sure I think very clearly around him. He has an effect on me. Better safe than sorry, right?" She felt the heat rising in her cheeks. He distracted her like no other.

"Well, I think it's smart." She gave her a warm smile. "Not that I think I'll find anything too salacious, considering I have most of his background completed, but let me do one more pass and write it up for you. But don't worry; I've got your back. I'll get it to you before you're discharged."

Despite Selena's encouragement, she still felt a little guilty for looking into Luke's past. Should she have just told Selena to forget it? She loved Luke and she trusted him. But then again, she never thought her brother-in-law would try to kill her either. She was mostly confident she was doing the right thing.

Her love for Luke was red-hot. She didn't want to be blinded by that passion and that desire. She needed someone like Selena to make sure she wasn't sprinting off a cliff into a sea of future devastation.

Kendall said, "Thank you. For everything. But there's something else I want to ask you about. How did you get into this private investigative work?"

Selena let out a deep exhale. "That's kind of a long story. Why?"

"I've been thinking about what's happened over the last year in my own life and contemplating my career, and then I saw you and all the good that you do. It made me think that maybe I should be doing something else, something more like you."

Selena looked skeptical. "You want to be a private investigator?"

"I don't know if that's it. But I want to help people. You help people. I make people richer. Don't get me wrong. I like working in finance, but it doesn't provide me with the purpose I feel I need. I started thinking a different occupation could do that. Throughout this ordeal, I've contemplated what would've happened if I hadn't had the money to hire a good lawyer or a good investigative team. Where would I be today? I'd probably be in jail, or worse, dead. What if I could help people who didn't have means? Or doing something that made a difference in people's lives?"

Selena said, "You want to have a career that gives back. That's great. Maybe you could be on the board of a charity or work for a nonprofit?"

Kendall shook her head. "No, I don't want to just sit on a board or be on the sideline when other people are doing the real work. I want to be the one who's out there helping. Throughout the investigation into George's death and into my own defense, I felt like I was pushed off to the side, helpless. I don't want to be helpless anymore. I want to be empowered. I want to be strong. I want to help other people. I want to be a doer. I see that in you, Selena. And that's why I thought I'd ask you for advice."

Selena glanced out the window and back at Kendall. "I hear what you're saying. There has been something I've been working on. I don't want to give too many details right now, but there might be something you could do to help. Give me some time to put together a more coherent plan. We'll keep in touch during your recovery, and when you're fully cleared to work, we can discuss details."

Kendall's eyes lit up. "Really? What is it? You can't even give me a hint? Pretty please."

Selena chuckled. "I don't want to give away too much right now, since it's still in the formation stages in my mind. I fear it may be incomprehensible to other humans right now. But I promise, as I have a clearer picture, we'll talk. I'll want your input on the plans. I think it's something, something that could be great. We'll keep in touch. Don't worry, Kendall, I won't forget about you. First, let's work on getting you back to 100 percent strength. Sound good?"

"Sounds great."

Kendall wondered why Selena couldn't tell her more details. She was dying to know. What could it be? Whatever it was, Kendall had a feeling it would be a life-changer.

CHAPTER THIRTY-SEVEN

KENDALL

Monday morning, Kendall studied the screen as she munched on fries in the hospital cafeteria. A grin spread across her face when she read the last lines in the summary section: *Kendall, you found one of the good ones. I hope Luke and you are very happy together.* She glanced across the table at Selena, who was busy picking at her green salad. "Do you always put in the summary whether or not he's a good guy?"

Selena chuckled. "Not usually. But I do want to point out that you definitely got one of the good ones. Luke seems like a great guy, and he obviously loves you. A lot of women aren't so lucky." Selena's smile melted away as she turned away and stared at the cucumber impaled on her fork.

Had Selena been one of the unlucky? She had been adamant that women should always get background checks on prospective partners, and her latest statement made Kendall wonder. Kendall didn't want to pry, but she was curious. She was also potentially going into business with Selena. It'd be nice to have a better picture of who she was as a person and what was important to her. "What do you mean, some aren't so lucky?" Kendall watched Selena's expression.

The PI glanced up and gave a reassuring smile, but there was sadness behind her eyes. "You'd be surprised how many monsters are out there, walking around, fooling everyone into believing they're good. Did you know that one in four women experience relationship violence in their lifetime? Intimate partner violence is so much more common than the general public realizes. That's why . . ." Selena stopped.

"That's why, what?"

Selena sighed. "Why I want to start a foundation to help women affected by domestic violence, and maybe even do community outreach to stop the violence before it starts. I didn't want to bring it up yet, because the concept is still just ideas floating around in my mind."

"Is this the opportunity you were telling me about—that maybe I could help with?" Kendall hoped so.

Selena nodded. "It's something that has been in the back of my mind for the last several years. I lost my mother to intimate partner violence. I want to start a foundation in her memory and to help other women and children, so they don't end up like she did. At the time, I didn't understand domestic violence very well, but over the years, the more I learned, the more I wanted to take action and try to make a difference. So when you mentioned wanting to have a job where you were helping people, I thought maybe it was something you might be interested in."

Kendall sat back and contemplated what Selena had told her. Was it true that one in four women would become victims of relationship violence in their lifetime? That was awful. Why didn't she know that? Kendall had never been a victim of abuse, other than of course her brother-in-law trying to kill her. Sadly, she didn't know the first thing about how to help victims of domestic violence, but she had a feeling Selena did. "What type of services for these women are you envisioning?"

Selena popped open her laptop. "I brainstormed different aspects I want to address. Let's see. Okay. Bear with me." She began to type. "Legal aid, help create safe-leaving plans, security services and protection, re-housing assistance, job assistance, education assistance, temporary shelter, community outreach, and self-defense."

Kendall's eyes widened. "If I understand correctly, you'd like to have a center for women, where they can go if they are currently in an abusive relationship, and provide both short-term and long-term support in order for them to leave safely while giving them the best chance for making a new life for themselves, *as well as* perform community outreach to educate others on domestic violence to help avoid it before it begins, correct?"

Selena's eyes sparkled. "That's exactly what I want to do. You said it perfectly. Maybe you and I should brainstorm ways of putting it all together. I mean, that is, if this is something you're interested in being a part of?"

Kendall thought aloud, "It'll be no small undertaking. We would need facilities, staff, specialists, lawyers, accountants, and frankly, *a lot* of money." Kendall took a deep breath in and then exhaled. This was huge. She grinned. "I would absolutely want to be a part of it."

Selena's excitement was palpable. Her whole face lit up. "Are you sure? It'll be a lot of work. I'm not sure if just the two of us could do it. I mean—like you said, we need—well, everything. I can teach the self-defense, and my firm could provide security and protection. I was thinking we could start small and then later expand."

"I agree it'll take a lot of planning and resources." Kendall paused. "As far as financial resources, I'd love to provide a large donation in George's name. It's likely enough to get the foundation started and running for a while. In parallel, we could look at fundraising opportunities to keep it going."

Selena's eyes welled with tears. "Are you serious?"

"Yes."

Selena slid out of her chair and walked over to Kendall and bent over to give her a hug. She said, "Thank you."

Selena stood back. Kendall shook her head. "No. Thank you, Selena. I can't wait to get started."

Selena dabbed her eyes with her napkin and sat back down. "You're not exactly healed yet. We should wait until you've been given the 'all clear' from the docs."

"We could still meet and plan. Also, so you know, I want to learn how to help these women and their families—not just be a facilitator. We'll need to factor that in, okay?"

"Of course. I can get you in shape when you're ready and then train you in self-defense so you can help teach. And then . . . oh, so many details to work out!"

"Yes, there are. It's such a great idea. I'm sure your mother would be really proud of you."

Tears filled Selena's eyes. "Kendall, when I first met you, I had a feeling we were brought together for a reason. That may sound weird, but I did. I felt the connection as soon as we met. I can feel it in my bones - this is going to be the beginning of something amazing."

Kendall grinned. "I feel it too."

CHAPTER THIRTY-EIGHT

FOUR WEEKS LATER, KENDALL

Kendall threw her head back and laughed. "Oh, Beth, please don't ever change." She glanced over her friend's shoulder and saw Grandma and Janine approaching. Dashing over to them, she flung her arms around both of them for a group hug. "I'm so happy to see both of you."

Grandma's pale-green eyes glittered. "And you too, my dear. It looks like you're doing well. I'm happy to see that. Oh, and your hair is growing back."

Janine teased. "I don't know. I kind of liked the partially shaved look. Very edgy."

Kendall shrugged. "I'm using less shampoo, so that's something." She was happy to be surrounded by her friends and family. She wanted to shout from the rooftops when the doctor gave her the 'all clear.'

She'd been blessed to not have sustained any permanent brain damage or cognitive issues related to her attack. She felt healthy and was getting stronger every day, thanks to Selena and her training plan. Kendall was determined to get fit and become the strongest version of herself she could be.

"Where's the booze?" Janine asked with a smile.

"I think Luke had the caterers put it in the dining room. Just follow the scent of whiskey, citrus, and Luxardo cherries. There's plenty, so help yourself."

Janine turned to Grandma. "C'mon, Grandma, let's get a drink! I'm ready to party."

Grandma pursed her bright magenta lips at Kendall. "How can I resist that kind of enthusiasm?"

Kendall chortled. "I don't think you can."

She heard the knock on the door of Luke's penthouse. It was as if everybody was arriving at the same time. *How many people did Luke invite?*

When Luke had suggested they throw a 'Kendall's back' party, she thought it was a little silly, but now she was glad he had persisted. She felt great, and like Janine, she was ready to party. Not too hard though. She was in training, but a little fun wouldn't hurt.

Luke walked into the living room with Detective Rogers. Uncharacteristically, Marcus was wearing a pair of blue jeans and white button-down shirt. She hadn't noticed until now, but Janine had been right. He was a bit of a detective hottie. Not that she had eyes for anyone other than Luke. Who knows, now that the case was over, maybe Marcus and Janine would get together. Janine had ogled him from day one. Wouldn't that be something?

She said, "I'm so glad you could make it." She gave Marcus a friendly hug. "How are you? It's good to see you in a non-official capacity."

Marcus frowned.

Uh-oh.

He lowered his voice. "There's been a development. I hate to discuss this at your party, but it's time-sensitive, as I fear it will be public knowledge soon."

Luke put his hand on her lower back and said, "Why don't we go into my office."

They walked solemnly to the modern-styled room with views of the Bay Bridge. Kendall's heart raced. "What is it?"

Marcus folded his arms across his chest. "They found Howard Davis murdered in his cell yesterday morning."

Kendall put her hand across her heart. "Oh my God. Who would do that? I mean, he's not my favorite person, but . . ." *But, it wasn't fair. He deserved to rot in prison. Death was too good for Howard.*

"This is where it gets hazy. Another inmate was the culprit, but according to witnesses, there had been no altercations between the two. His murder is assumed to be a prison hit. Gates and I took a trip to visit Irwin Dratch. He wasn't too forthcoming, but he did allude to the fact that he'd never received final payment from Howard and how 'when one doesn't keep their word, there are consequences.' We'll never get a confession or a prosecution, but it's something."

Kendall's mouth fell open. "Dratch hired someone to kill Howard because he didn't receive final payment for killing George?"

Marcus said, "Looks like it."

Kendall turned to Luke. "That's crazy, right?"

Luke nodded.

She faced Marcus again. "So, then it's over. All of it. No trial."

He gave a sheepish grin. "That's right."

It's really over. Tears filled her eyes. "Thank you."

Luke grabbed Kendall's hand and pulled her into a hug. She wiped her eyes and stepped back. "What do you say we rejoin the party?"

Marcus grinned. "Sounds like a great idea."

Luke said, "Agreed."

Back in the party zone, Luke and Kendall joined Janine, Grandma, and Beth, all of whom held pink cocktails in their hands. Luke said it was Kendall's signature drink. "Hey, ladies," Kendall said.

Janine sipped. "It's the woman of the hour. How goes it?"

"A bit of news." She explained about Howard and a darkness planted in her gut.

Beth said, "I'll drink to that," and downed the rest of her cosmopolitan.

Their laughter was interrupted by a knock at the door. Was it terrible to be smiling when a man, a former family member, was dead? Luke squeezed her and gave her a kiss before pulling back and saying, "I'll get it."

More friends and former coworkers arrived. The party was getting rowdy and cheerful. Unquestionably a celebration. Yet a pit began growing in her stomach. She snuck out of the room and made her way to the master bedroom. She was happy and excited about her new life, but sadness remained. So much loss in such a short amount of time.

The home she'd built with George was in escrow, and Eleanor Davis had passed away three weeks earlier. Between the house being sold, Eleanor, and now Howard, all of her connections to George were gone. It was the final chapter in a life she had once loved. A life where she had a loving and stable husband. A life where she felt safe. Untouchable. A life where she was going to be a mother and go to soccer games and karate lessons. The American dream. It was a beautiful vision. The vision was fuzzy now. After all of it, she could never go back to a life like that.

It struck her that the party was simultaneously an end and a beginning.

She walked over to the window, pulled back the shade, and stared out at the clear, blue sky. "George, if you're out there, please know I love you and I will never forget you." Her voice cracked, and she allowed the tears to fall. And fall.

She jerked around at the sound of the door opening. She sighed in relief. "Hi, Grandma."

Grandma approached with arms outstretched. Kendall cried into her grandma's embrace. After a while, she pulled back and wiped the tears with the back of her hands. "What's wrong, my sweet?" Grandma asked.

"I don't know." Kendall shook her head. "That's not true. I do know. I'm torn. I love and miss George, but . . ."

"You're in love with Luke."

Kendall averted her gaze and nodded. Since she'd been staying with Luke over the last month, she had fallen even harder for him. Something she hadn't thought was possible. Had she become too accustomed to waking up next to him each morning? Not that there was a plan for her to move out, but there wasn't a plan for her to stay either.

The idea of being without Luke caused physical pain in her chest. She had learned the hard way with George, that if you love someone, they can be taken from you in an instant. Should she throw caution to the wind and tell him exactly how she was feeling? She didn't want him out of her life ever again. She didn't want to leave him. She wanted to live with him, permanently, and wanted a future with him, but something inside of her kept pulling her back. Was it guilt? Fear?

Grandma took Kendall's hands into hers. They were so soft and warm. "Kendall dear, you and George shared a great love. It's so unfair and cruel that he was taken away from you. You will always have a place in your heart for George. Loving Luke won't change that. George would have been grateful that you found a new love, a love who loves and supports you. It's okay to love Luke—and it's okay to start a new life with him."

"You don't think it's too soon?"

"Does he make you happy?"

She nodded.

"Do you want to have a life with him?"

She nodded.

"Then no, it's not. Don't hold back. Take life by the balls, Kendall."

"Grandma!" She sniffled through her smile.

"You only get one life. Do what makes you happy."

Kendall hugged her grandma, inhaling her lavender perfume. "Thank you, Grandma."

"Anytime. Are you okay now?"

"Yeah, I think so."

"Great, I really need to find the bathroom. I thought this was the bathroom."

Kendall gave her directions to the guest bathroom and wondered if Grandma had gotten lost because of the dementia. She shook her head in an attempt to throw out the idea. She couldn't face that right now.

Kendall entered the master bathroom and dotted her eyes with a tissue, reapplied her makeup, and rejoined the party.

She called out to Luke, who was heading down the hall toward the front door. "I'll get it." She opened the door and a wide grin crept up her face. "Selena, I'm so glad you made it. "

"I wouldn't have missed it for the world." As she stepped over the threshold, Kendall hugged her.

Over the last few weeks, Kendall and Selena had grown very close. Despite her younger age, Selena had become somewhat of a mentor, and soon they would be partners.

Selena said, "Love that dress."

"This old thing?" Kendall hadn't worn anything fancier than jogging pants or athleisure attire over the last month. She had decided to put on a sparkly fit-and-flare dress paired with a low heel for the party.

She led Selena to the rest of the group, who appeared to be having a great time laughing, chatting, eating, and drinking. She walked with Selena over to Marcus and Gates. She paused and watched as Marcus's eyes lit up at the sight of Selena. She glanced at Selena, who had the same twinkle in her eyes. It was that shiny, fixated look, as if they didn't realize there were other people in the room. How had she not seen it before?

Luke handed Selena a flute. "Now that Selena has arrived, I think it's time for a toast." Luke handed Kendall a glass as well.

With one arm around her waist, he said, "Now that everyone has a glass of champagne . . ." He raised his and turned to Kendall. "I'm elated that you're healthy and happy and here with us today. I love you and am excited for what the future may bring."

Lots of whispers from the crowd. Kendall's heart pounded. *He's not.*

"Cheers!"

Phew.

Kendall took a sip of the bubbly and was greeted with a sweet and spicy kiss from Luke. He whispered, "I love you."

It's time to be brave again. "Hey, can we talk for a minute?"

Luke said, "Of course."

Kendall grabbed his hand and led him back into the master bedroom. "I want to talk to you about something."

Sitting on the bed, he grabbed her hips and pulled her close. "Is 'talk' code for something else?"

She grinned stupidly at him. "No, you pervert. I wanted to talk to you about us."

He grew serious. "Yeah?"

"Now that I'm healthy and don't *have* to stay with you."

His eyes grew wide. "You want to move out?"

She bit her lower lip and shook her head.

He grinned, and her heart melted.

"Is that okay?" she asked.

"Let's call the movers and get the rest of your stuff from storage." He pulled out his phone. "I'll call right now."

She giggled and grabbed it from his hands. "You're quite silly, Luke Abbington. You know, I love that about you."

"Is that so? Well, I try to please. Was there anything else you wanted to talk about?"

"Nope."

"So, can we do other stuff now?"

"We have guests out there!"

He pouted. "Fine. Later."

She gave him a quick peck, and they headed back out to the party, hand in hand. Yes, it was definitely time to be brave.

THANK YOU!

Thank you for reading *A Permanent Mark*! I hope you enjoyed reading it as much as I loved writing it. If you did, I would greatly appreciate if you could post a short review.

Reviews are crucial for any author and can make a huge difference in visibility of current and future works. Reviews allow us to continue doing what we love, *writing stories*. Not to mention, I would be forever grateful!

To leave a review, go to the sales page from whichever store you purchased *A Permanent Mark* from and write away!

Thank you!

ALSO BY H.K. CHRISTIE

The Selena Bailey Series is a suspenseful series featuring a young Selena Bailey and her turbulent path to becoming a top notch kickass private investigator.

Not Like Her, Book 1

One In Five, Book 2

On The Rise, Book 3

The Unbreakable Series is a heart-warming women's fiction series, inspired by true events. If you like journeys of self-discovery, wounded heroines, and laugh-or-cry moments, you'll love the Unbreakable series.

We Can't Be Broken, Book 0

Where I'm Supposed To Be, Book 1

Change of Plans, Book 2

JOIN H.K. CHRISTIE'S READER CLUB

Join my reader club to be the first to hear about upcoming novels, new releases, giveaways, promotions, and more!

It's completely free to sign up and you'll never be spammed by me, you can opt out easily at any time.

Sign up today at
www.authorhkchristie.com

ABOUT THE AUTHOR

H.K. Christie is the author of compelling stories featuring unbreakable women.

When not working on her latest novel, she can be found eating & drinking with friends, running slowly, or playing with her rescue pup, Mr. Buddy Founders.

She is a native and current resident of the San Francisco Bay Area and a two time graduate of Saint Mary's College of California.

www.authorhkchristie.com

ACKNOWLEDGMENTS

I'd like to thank my family and friends (especially the mister) for all the encouragement and support in getting this book out into the world.

In addition, I'd like to thank my super, developmental editor, Dawn Husted for the thoughtful comments and suggestions. You're awesome. Thank you to Brooks Becker for the copy edit. Thank you to Suzana Stankovic who designed the cover. You did an amazing job with the cover - as you always do. Thank you!

Made in the USA
Coppell, TX
29 March 2022